DEATH'S

STALKER

Death's Stalker

Copyright © 2022 by Stephanie Gluck

All rights reserved.

ISBN Paperback: 978-0-6454075-5-6
ISBN: Electronic: 978-0-6454075-4-9

For Rhys, who I will love in every realm.

&

Mr. Puff, always.

Also by Stephanie Gluck:

THE DEVIL'S TRIALS

Feast of Samael

Heist of Haures

Ire of War

Tower of Hubris

Dreams of Sin

Festival of Hearts

THE FOUR REALMS

Death's Stalker

Death's Stalker
Content Advisory

Please note that this book is a fantasy romance containing dark themes and has been written for an intended audience over the age of 18 years.

This book contains themes pertaining to death, coercion, and sexually explicit content that some readers may not find comfortable.

For further information on the themes and content of this book, please visit: www.stephaniegluck.com/trigger-warnings

Death's Stalker

The Four Realms

Stephanie Gluck

Prologue:

Keziah

She lost the soft, pink slipper as it fell from her heel, precious seconds wasted as the girl had to pause to retrieve it in the race to get them down as quickly as possible. Carefully pinned tendrils of hair fell loose from the pins at the nape of her neck, and by the time Keziah reached the ground floor, they bounced around her face. Soft curls turned and uncontrolled, brushed against the side of her face, tickling her nose until she sneezed.

It was at that sound that her mother whirled from her place in the doorway. Stormy eyes narrowed on the youngest of her two daughters, and beneath that stare, Keziah wilted. Her will to stand up to the queen was akin to a dandelion, loosened and lost in a soft wind. She did not have the strong, sunflower spine of her sister, Kalani.

Side by side, the princesses of the Quaver Court were similar. Keziah had been born only eleven short months after Kalani, but sometimes it felt like a lifetime separated them. They both had soft heart-shaped faces, russet skin, and eyes the colour of ancient sea storms, but that was where the comparison ended. It often was the Queen's greatest joy to point out that a second daughter, even a princess, was worth extraordinarily little among the sirens. She reminded her daughter of it, frequently.

Even by seven years old, Keziah knew she paled compared to her sister. She would never be as pretty, she would never say the right things, and she would never, ever have the same power. There was immense power in being the heir to the Quaver sirens and Keziah would be lucky to taste even a drop it of it in her lifetime.

"What are you doing here?" The Queen hissed. Even in anger her voice was melodious, the rise and fall of allure itself.

Keziah swallowed, her small fingers pushing a soft curl from her face. She was suddenly acutely aware of how Kalani's hair stayed pinned nicely in place.

"I'm coming to the party!" She chirped.

Instantly, she could see that had been the wrong thing to say. The Queen's face clouded with displeasure, the storm in her eyes expanding to the tightening of her lips, cording the muscles in her neck.

The Carnality Court was visiting, and Keziah had been waiting impatiently all day for festivities to begin, but Queen Kalliah offered her such a dark look that the little girl shrank back. Disappointment weighed heavily on her heart. She knew, before they said anything, that her mother would deny her entrance to the festivities. Once again, she would miss out.

"My Queen," Keziah's father, King Consort Nevian, stepped forward to place an arm on the Queen's forearm. His smile was soft and placating, a grin like spun sugar, sought by all. He had no power in the Quaver Court and only an honorary title, but he did not flinch beneath the frightening power in his wife's expression. "We don't want to be late."

Keziah's heart skipped a beat, feeling the soft edge of disappointment that he hadn't insisted for her to come, too.

The Queen drew a breath, filling her lungs, and fixed a smile in place. It was rigid and perfect, but utterly fake.

"Take Kalani and go in, my dear. The Carnality Queen will understand." Her eyes remained fixed on the little girl. "I must have a word with our youngest daughter."

Keziah looked to her father, grey eyes wide with silent and desperate appeal. He glanced down at the seven-year-old standing in her sister's dress. His gaze turned sad, the lines in his face grim, and Keziah's lower lip wobbled into a pout.

The King Consort, her father, would not save her from her mother.

"Go on! Take Kalani into the party and leave us be!" The Queen's voice had taken on a familiar edge. It was soft and coaxing, heavily laced with the power it had afforded her as the first-born daughter in a royal siren line.

They were children of mixed blood, born of the ancient Fae and underwater Mer-people, two races that should not have merged. The sirens had been born with power so great that they had overwhelmed Solis entirely, taking their places in kingdoms and claiming land for themselves. Their queens held great power and bequeathed down to the females of their courts. Power that Kalani shared and would one day control completely, of which Keziah possessed only a drop.

It was, as always, brutally swift and effective. The Queen's voice slid past the King Consort's mental defences and the command took root in his mind. His dark eyes glazed with the edge of a thought that was not his own, and Nevian turned to reach for Kalani, holding out his soft hand.

"Come, darling." He called.

Kalani nodded, always so serious and unwilling to intervene. She reached for her father's hand solemnly. They swept out through the last chamber and into the festivities beyond.

As the door opened, Keziah could hear the hum, laughter, and conversation. When it closed and left them in foreboding silence, she felt the first flutter of nerves in her belly. The seven-year-old fisted her hands behind her back, twisting them into the buttery fabric of her dress and waited, staring down at her jewelled slippers.

"Look at me, Keziah."

The command took hold. Magic was an icy cold in her mind that stretched out across her nerves, mobilising her limbs, and forcing action.

Keziah's chin tipped up, cherub cheeks and long dark lashes turned towards her Queen, for it was the Queen invading her mind with sacred insurmountable power, and not her mother, who should have loved her more than that, but never did.

"Yes, Mama." There was no melody to her child-soft voice, only the thready bray of fear. The wish that the term of endearment might give her pause.

"Yes, *my queen*."

The correction was swift, along with the sharp crack of the Queen's hand across her face. Keziah's head snapped to the side on impact. She blinked against sudden tears and stinging pain.

"*Look at me, Keziah*." The queen demanded again, giving her no time to process it, no time to cry.

Keziah's attention turned back to the Queen. Regardless of whether she wanted to, her body would obey the power. The Quaver Court, the deadliest of the three Siren powers, allowed for influence and removal of free will. The sirens' song was not a suggestion, but a command.

The burning mark on Keziah's skin felt like it was glowing beneath the Queen's inspection. Time seemed to suspend before Queen Kalliah clicked her tongue disapprovingly, as if Keziah had marked herself just to be contrary.

Her hand tugged at her skirts, pulling the hem from the ground, and Queen Kalliah dropped to her knees, levelling at Keziah's height for the first time in her life.

The child blinked, confused; she shrank back, unsure of the protocol that followed.

"*Keziah*," the queen laced power in her daughter's name. She reached up, slender fingers adjusting the crooked placement of the silver diadem that signified that the child was one of royal blood. Tension coiled between the woman and her child. Keziah shivered at the sound of her name, trapped and waiting.

"*You are the spare of Quaver Court, the second daughter, the forgotten princess. You do not represent us. You do not attend parties and make a name for yourself. You do not step into your sister's spotlight. She has the power of our people, not you.*" The Queen sung. "*You will go upstairs; you will remain out of the way. You will be seen and not heard unless I tell you otherwise.*"

The siren commands washed over Keziah like an icy rain; it was not refreshing, but chilling. Her entire body trembled as it processed the magic that poured from the queen to the youngest daughter. It wrapped around her free will and bound it tight, layered atop of older strands of magic and secured like bands of iron.

Queen Kalliah lifted her chin, glancing down her nose at the child, impatiently brushing a soft curl from her daughter's face. "*Tell me you understand, Princess Keziah of Quaver.*"

Not a question, another command.

Keziah's heart raced and her lips shifted without her own conscious design. "I understand."

The queen's jewelled fingers pinched at her chin, a sharp flare of pain in reprimand. "I understand, *my queen.*"

Keziah parroted the words back, quickly, desperately, sagging with relief when the Queen cleared her throat and the thick feeling of magic in the room slipped away.

The Queen stood. Easily forgetting the child at her side, and turning her attention to the party beyond, she focussed on the courts that awaited her arrival.

Keziah turned without a word and followed the command to go upstairs and wait out the days of festivity. Queen Kalliah was a song-siren, the nineteenth generation of royal blood with the strength to show for it.

The words she sang would remain with her daughter forever. A pretty and powerful curse.

Prologue:

Death

Traditionally, fae males did not come to their powers until they survived childhood, since so many younglings perished before they could walk. Elemental power triggered at the first mating when instinct overcame the last vestiges of their control. After millennia of infighting, only two Fae territories remained across Solis, while their Mer counterparts and Siren children had gained control of the land, after they sought to find their independence and their place in what was once a fae ruled world. The Sirens had overtaken them, three queen led courts of arrogance and pride, but they let their fae ancestors be.

The Fae divided themselves neatly into two camps. All Fae belonged in one or the other without question.

Argent and Ash: the territories of Chaos and Calm.

The Argent Fae were known for their reckless natures and impulsive decision making. They were quick to enter a fight and unbelievably competitive. They trained warriors without fear. Their children were born with affinities of wind and fire and learned to wield them as weapons. Hot tempered and passionate, the Argents would march into battle without question.

The Ash Fae were known for a more balanced mental capacity. They made rational and well thought out decisions, ensuring keen and informed political moves. Their children were born with control of waters and the grass, used to further their territory and stifle the supply of their enemies. Their elders ran the governments and designed the covenants of Solis that allow three races to live together.

All children in the Ash territory lived together until they came into their own power. There were no parents to create rash decision making or competitiveness, no nurturing, just education. They were wards of the state, in the design to allow babes to grow with a wealth of information and the hopes they would remain aligned to Ash.

They raised him as an Ash fae. A serious child with honeysuckle eyes and a noted absent smile, as if he knew a secret that he would never tell, but that amused him always.

He had not been the most intelligent of the children; he was not pleasant, and could not talk his way in circles like the best of the politicians. With so little going for him, there had been high hopes that when his first mating came, he would have a strong affinity and natural power, because he had been decidedly lacking in every other area.

His first mating took a long time to come. Not that he minded, even as friends awoke and found their gifts and their places in the world. He had always been content to wait; he did not like change.

In the late spring of his twenty-seventh year, he woke mid-morning in a frenzy of emotion, coated in slick sweat and trembled with uncontrollable magic and hormones.

He felt utterly wild. He felt free. He tumbled a fae female in the soft grass beside the lake, a rough, fumbling rut to fulfil a need, caring not when she disappeared shortly after and left him alone in his dulling emotions.

He stared up at the canopies, idling over whether that was truly the pathetic moment when his entire life would change for the better.

The mating was passionate, but not what he had expected. Elders had always spun tales of the importance of a fae's first mating and the call to elemental power. It was a rite of passage, and a coming of age. It had only left him exhausted. She had been soft, eager and he would do it again, but he didn't feel it had changed his life. There had been no electricity or fire beneath his skin, the flowers had not bloomed, a tornado hadn't appeared at his climax. She had been wet, willing, intense, but she had not been magical. She had ignited nothing inside him.

Exhaustion claimed him. His eyes fluttered closed. In the soft seconds between consciousness and sleep, the male lost his grip on the plane of his existence, and he fell through one realm and landed the next.

The human realm was noisy. He landed on a hard bitumen, and it scraped against his naked skin. There was a symphony of screeching brakes and tyres as a large metal beast swerved, barely missing him. The fae male jumped to his feet, bitter adrenaline raising bile to the back of his tongue. He grasped at the drawstrings of his pants to cover himself and fled from the next metal beast that raced to meet him, as the beasts kept coming, hurtling down this hard path with only a flash of warning light that half blinded him.

Strange people leaned out of them, their ears oddly rounded, and screamed in a language he didn't understand. The violence of their tones left him cringing. He didn't need to understand their tongue to understand their anger.

He twisted on the spot, searching for any evidence of the bubbling stream of familiar fields he had been in, and found only cold stone and flashing lights. Building that stretched, without character, into the sky.

More beings came into view, hurrying down the path. They milled about like ants in a rush to find food scurrying this way and that. He could feel the flicker of their eyes against his skin, inspecting, judgemental and some spat words that meant nothing but sounded too loud with his acute hearing.

This place was so loud, and his head spun for it. He ran, feeling foolish for being so frightened after over two decades of life and having finally left his juvenility behind.

He twisted around the corner, the fae curses on his lips. He fell through the realms again.

Shadowed monsters crawled out from the dark, luminous eyes fixed on him, hungry and mesmerised. Where he had been running in one direction, the male skidded to a stop, slipping along the ground. Every muscle in his body clenched at the danger in front of him. It blinked with deep violet eyes and swirling shadows.

He crouched low, defensive, baring his teeth.

"Well, well.... A visitor." A feminine voice purred through the night.

A female stepped forward, and the shadows parted for her, the demons shifting out of her way. She had sharp, black nails, gleaming red eyes, and pointed teeth.

She smiled, and he bared his teeth back at her with a growl of warning that rumbled from deep within his pale chest. The female had a wreath of snakes that coiled and hissed around her crown, growing from her head. The soft light bounced off shining gold scales that covered her skin, likening her to them.

"Stay away!" He warned.

"A fae male!" She laughed and each of those snakes around her head swayed at the sound. "How yummy!"

She reached for him, catching him even as he spun away, her claws dragging down his arm. The skin split, tearing a cry from his throat, and black shadows poured from the cuts and into the realm, curling around his skin in claim of him.

The world tilted, and he landed in Solis again.

He landed in a familiar place, the large stone buildings of the town square, covered with slow growing ivy and filled with fae that he had known his entire life; but at the sight of him, blinking into existence out of nothing, they all came to a sharp faces and sharper gazes all on him. He stood, tense and weary. He would have called it a dream, but blood and wisps of shadow still streamed down his right forearm, the gouges from the snake wreathed demoness' nails split open across his skin.

Dark shadows wreathed his hands, curling around his fingers and sliding up his wrists.

One of the fae elders, one of the oldest still living, Elder Raahn, approached him slowly. The old male had his hands raised in a placating manner; his expression was carefully blank.

The fae male observed him. He knew Elder Raahn was a Master of Water, particularly pulling moisture from the air. In times of war, he was rumoured to have pulled every ounce of water from his enemies' bodies,

"Come, son." The elder commanded. "We must talk."

He frowned. "I am not your son."

"Indeed," Elder Raahn agreed. "You are no son of Ash at all. Therefore, we must discuss your eviction."

His heartbeat seemed to slow as comprehension loomed. "What did you say?"

"You heard me, child." Elder Raahn straightened. Other fae filtered out of the square, not willing to be in the path of conflict. Such was the way of the Ash.

"This is my home. I live here," He stated, a thread of panic stark in his tone. "I belong here."

The elder shook his head, jerking his chin at the male's shadow wreathed hands as if it were explanation enough. "Leave to the wildlands of Solis and take your own life in any manner you want, or I will execute you on the spot."

It was no idle threat. Elder Raahn did not make jokes.

He set his jaw. "I'll go to Argent."

"They won't take you," the elder stated. "Our territories fight at times, but we agree on one thing above all others. Corrupted fae are not permitted to live."

"I am not corrupted."

"No fae of the sun, moon nor darkness shall live." Elder Raahn spoke the same words he had heard throughout his entire childhood, a message ingrained in his soul. "Which do you think you are?"

His head spun, not from the words of his elder, but the way the world was tipping out of focus again. Panic flared through him, hot and then cold, and he tried to grasp at the threads of his own reality. It was useless though, and he shifted, uncontrolled and unwilling, into the fourth realm.

T he final realm was a vast and empty space. Alone as the shadows liked a path up his forearms, and threatened to overtake him completely. He twisted on the spot, staring across the empty fields and into the storm laden sky above him. The clouds rolled, angry and grey.

"Take me back!" He roared to the skies.

Nothing happened.

The male raced, one way and the other, running until he had no energy left. He twisted and twirled, doing everything he could to push back through whatever veils had fallen through to get back to Solis.

It was futile. He remained in the empty plane alone and exhausted, tumbling into soft grass with growled curses.

Time had no real measure there; where he did not hunger or have normal needs. He didn't know if he lay in that grass for one day or one year. He could have aged a lifetime, forgotten by all who once knew him.

It changed when one day, from a distance, two figures approached him. They were two parts of one whole.

One wreathed in darkness, and the other in light.

He leapt to his feet and attacked them. Sensing a threat, he shot forward with bared teeth and swinging fists. He launched himself at them with what felt like a lifetime of accumulated rage.

They exchanged looks, and laughed, as they slipped easily out of the way, dancing around him in both directions.

"The prophecy was true," the light one laughed as he pulled himself upright, watching them wearily, gaze flickering to work out the best method to attack. "It's him."

They closed in around him and the one wreathed in light reached for his arm, cold hands pressed over the gouges in his skin. They had long since stopped bleeding, but the skin had never healed over. Beneath the light wreathed fingers, shining scars formed, pink and agitated, but knit together at last.

"What prophecy?" He hissed, wrenching his arm back.

The dark one let out a noise of glee at his pain, its eyes flaring with a deep, violent power.

"Hmm,' The light one hummed.

"He's a bit grim, isn't he?" the dark one commented.

They both laughed.

"What prophecy?" The fae male repeated in an angry hiss, his irritation building the longer they ignored him. He leapt for the light one, barely missing them and rolling across the ground as the darkness shifted, forming into a creature with looming wings. He laughed loudly, a sound that cracked across the open fields.

"Death has finally come home to us."

1

Relief was the only thing Keziah felt when her mother's chest stopped moving. When the gasping rattle of the woman's futile attempts to cling to life finally stopped ringing through the room. It had been a long night of waiting for Queen Kalliah to give up on the magic that kept her alive, for the magic to abandon her, for the safety of a new queen instead. Keziah's older sister, Kalani, was now officially Queen of one of the three major siren courts, and she shattered the silence as she burst into noisy tears. Her chair toppled as she lurched forward and reached for the hands of mother and father. They lay still in bed, undertaking the last rest.

The new queen crawled onto the bed beside her parents' lifeless bodies. It was only then that Keziah realised her mother had pulled her father through to the grave with her, as selfish in death as she had been in all other aspects of life. He had not outlasted her by even a minute to enjoy life in his own right.

"Kala," Keziah needed to do something, anything, now that her elder sister had her arms wreathed around their father's cold shoulders. "Kalani, come on. You need to get down." She tugged at her sister's arm, forcing her backwards until they tumbled onto the carpeted floor.

Her sister spun, grief and rage twisting her normally beautiful features into something feral and hateful. "*Don't touch me!*" Kalani hissed the words, but they came out with an all too familiar lilt.

The words laced with more power than Keziah had ever felt from her sister before, they slipped beneath her carefully built mental defences and before Keziah knew what was happening, she had let go, careful not to brush against her sister at all.

"Kalani!" she gasped.

Once, long ago, the two sisters had sworn never to use their powers on one another like their mother did to others.

Even if the woman had tortured one more than the other, they both knew the feeling of having their free will and choices erased.

It was a promise that was easier for Keziah to keep who little power of her own except on the nights of the full moon, but until this day her sister had kept her word.

Now, everything had changed.

Kalani advanced in three quick steps until they were nose to nose. Two young women with the same umber skin and stormy grey eyes, long lashes, and full mouths, but where Kalani of Quaver lifted herself to her full height, Keziah wilted, making herself as small as she could.

"No," Kalani hissed. "You have always hated them, Kez. You don't mourn them, so you will not speak. You will stand to the side of the room and wait until I am ready for you."

Tears welled in Keziah's stormy eyes. The words, the biting tone. They weren't unfamiliar, but she had never heard the hardened edge in Kalani's voice. Her sister had always had a little compassion.

"Kala..."

"No." Kalani's skin shimmered, empowered by using her strengthened gifts, her magic feeding on the manipulation of her sister. Quaver Sirens always shined after the use of their gifts, healthier when they used their gifts, their natures fed on the manipulation of others. "Move aside and wait, Keziah."

Almost robotically, Keziah moved as her sister had ordered. She shuffled into the corner, a bitter hatred burning in the pit of her stomach, but the command had been to wait, so she couldn't move away until permission came, so she stared at the toes of her jewelled slippers and mulled over her misfortunes of being in such a place in court.

The Quaver Court of Solis was one of three main sects of Sirens that existed in the land: Quaver, Carnality, and Dreamous. Each was born from the same sect of magic in Solis, gifted from a cross-heritage of forbidden love.

Their magic fed when they manipulated others in their court. It was an effect particularly potent on humans, but other magical beings were also vulnerable if one held enough power. Usually only royal blood could manipulate another siren with lasting effect.

The sirens maintained a matriarchal power system. Queens were born in a direct line, and each queen birthed only two daughters in every generation.

Their heir and the spare.

The three queens held most of the power in their courts, very few people could deny the call of a queen. Their heirs came next strength and everyone else paled in comparison, even the spare.

The average siren possessed some power, enough to manipulate any humans that walked into Solis, but not enough to harm one another. It was enough to keep balance and peace, enough to make them the predator to human prey.

Keziah of Quaver had been born a spare.

Her power was present but severely limited by her position in the line of ascension. Occasionally she had got a serving girl to follow a magically charged suggestion and been able to feel the shimmer of magic, the pleasure of having fed, but her voice was unremarkable. She could never slip a suggestion into someone's mind in the same way that her sister did. Eyes would not glaze over at her soft tones, and obedience would not come easy.

Kalani, in comparison, now glowed with her satiated power. She turned away stiffly, her soft skirts fluttering around her ankles as she faced the bed and reached to hold their parents' stiff hands.

A soft, age-old prayer, whispered from her lips, laced with the siren song as if it might force it to come true, and Kalliah and Nevian would find peace in the next life. Kalani bowed her head over their bodies and whispered wishes over their bodies.

Keziah shifted uncomfortably. She tipped her chin up to stare at the cavernous, polished wooden ceiling and exposed beams of their parents' bedroom. The palace was a cold brick castle on the outside by the rich polished woods and plush carpets breathed warmth into the rooms.

She closed her eyes, pretending to pray, and tried to search her memory for a happy moment with the two. There were a few, with her father, King Consort, who had once been a gentle soul, but his mind left warped with as many rules and demands from the Queen as Keziah herself had suffered, and so his youngest daughter had not seen his warm smile in years.

It slipped away once there was more magic than the male in his actions. They were thoughtless obedience, not choices and indulgence.

Beyond that, she couldn't think of a happy memory of her mother. Keziah had seen her mother scowl in her direction more than she had smiled.

She knew why. They had reminded her, many times, that she was only a spare. Unnecessary, just as Queen Kalliah's sister Kierie had been, to be removed as soon as it was convenient.

Keziah had always known, throughout the course of her life, that as soon as Kalani ascended and birthed her first child, her own life would be forfeited. Spares could not live once the next heir breathed, their dimmed power was forfeit, and they would not be allowed to become a threat to the throne. They were simply insurance until their elder sisters took their place.

That was how Queen Kalliah, who had never truly been a mother, had always seen Keziah. It showed in the scars on her mind, where strict rules and barked demands, laced with magic that she couldn't deny. Cruses that bound her so tight that sometimes the young siren wondered if she had a mind of her own at all.

Keziah swallowed roughly and opened her eyes, thinking of one of those imposed restrictions. Queen Kalliah was dead, she realised, and her heart lifted with a moment of joy.

She could be free.

There were so many layers of magically bound restrictions, things Keziah wanted to do and could not, that it was all too easy to pick one to test out. At age nine, in a bout of temper, she had called her sister a 'sirret,' which was a common-person's term for a siren who whored herself out to mermen in exchange for jestweed. Sirret's were dazed people who wanted power in any way they could get it, even high with a slimy, scaled Mer.

It wasn't a word any nine-year-old princess should have known, and Keziah had picked it up from crude jokes between the guards when they hadn't known she was listening. Her mother had slapped her twice, and her tongue silenced with the Queens song. She could remember it well.

"You will never speak ill of your sister, Keziah."

Since then, the magic had shackled her, and Keziah had barely been able to complain when her sister annoyed her, let alone describe her in colourful or foul language.

Now, her tongue darted out to wet her full lips, her heartbeat racing with nerves and anticipation. She stared at the back of her sister's curly head, unable to move until she let her do so. Such were the intricacies of siren control.

"You are an absolute..." Her tongue caught on the word, stilling, and Keziah choked on it, choked on the magic that stilled her desire to spit curses at her sister, which wound tight and prevented it from happening.

Tears of frustration burned behind her eyes, and she glared at the dead body of Queen Kalliah. The woman who cursed her even after death.

"What did you say?" Kalani demanded, voice shrill but thankfully normal. It was a question she could refuse if she wanted.

Keziah swallowed down the words, and the thread of growing hatred for the Queen of Quaver, regardless of who it was that wore the crown. She closed her eyes and exhaled her rage in the face of her sister's obvious grief.

"Nothing, Kala," she sighed softly. "Nothing at all."

Keziah forced herself to still, to calm, and mourn the knowledge that with death nothing had changed.

2

After hundreds of years living in a realm where time did not move in any coherent manner, Death had long since settled into his new moniker and shifted between the four planes of reality with ease, stepping into places with more motion and rigidity than his own home. He was used to the fact that five years could pass in Zemē, a realm that evolved slower than his own. He was death.

The single soul who shifted from one realm to another in a manner that was as simple as stretching the muscles in his back, relaxing the worries in his mind, and moving on the next exhale through the realms until he ended up where the souls called for him.

He heard a litany of voices nobody else could hear, the whispered agony of the final plea of life.

Death was rigid in his routine. He had four realms to manage, more souls than could be comprehended by others.

The first realm, his realm, Iriya, was an ever-changing plane of shadows and quiet where Death ruled and the souls within could take one of three paths. Rest, rebirth, and recompense. Time moved differently here. His face of Death had existed now for twelve hundred and forty-three years, but he had aged only in the minutes that he returned to Solis. He looked barely older than the Fae boy had been when his shadows awoke, and his responsibilities began, the picture of the young fae male who wanted a purpose in the world.

Next came Kihnes, the Shadow Realm, where the shadows and the monsters of day and night devoured one another. Ruled by a gorgon by the name of Danye. Demons of all sires bowed down to her word and her rule.

The third plane had once been his home. Solis, a realm of magic, where the Fae had rejected him, the Sirens had claimed power and the Mer had begun to climb above the sea.

Finally, there was Zemē, a realm of humans. A place where the people had forgotten magic, where technology and the concept of science had taken its place. Even after all this time, it was still a strange and noisy place for Death to visit, where time moved slowly, the people felt disconnected, and their lives were too busy to appreciate what they had.

Death stepped through the realms into Solis, blinking rapidly as his eyes adjusted to the bright midday sun. There was tension coiling down his spine, and he took a moment to roll his shoulders and stretched.

He had stepped right into Quaver Castle, through a doorway nobody else could see. Young sirens flittered down the hall, heads bowed close, as they whispered softly about the deaths of their monarchs. The very same souls that had called him forth.

They scurried right past him. Theirs eyes did not flicker to where he stood, their attention not drawn in his direction. It was as if he was not there at all.

Death was a formidable presence, but he was and had long been invisible. It was how he preferred it.

He walked slowly through the castle. There was never a hurry, and sirens moved from his way, as if guided by an invisible force to mind his path.

Nobody liked to be in the presence of Death. It was a lonely occupation, but the souls of Iriya kept him company. He squared his shoulders and followed the call of the untethered souls. They released an energy that called to his own soul, a keening that only his ears could hear, as they cried for security once more.

Death's entire body slid through the solid bulk of the wooden doors as he stepped from the hall to the old queen's bedroom. There were two of them, still and vacant bodies laid in the bed, their daughter clinging to their hands as if she could keep them anchored in this realm.

Nobody could keep him from taking souls. No prayer or force of will was strong enough.

He stepped around the young mourning siren and leaned over the bed to inspect the Queen and King Consort. Death could see the bright core of their souls, settled in their chests, as they waited for him, their cries still echoing in his ears.

Death reached over the first of the bodies, his white hair falling forward and obscuring his face. His hand slipped through their flesh and bone, as easily as he walked through the walls, to coax the light from their chests.

The King Consort's soul shifted first. It reacted to the soft stroke of his fingertips, shivering beneath his touch before it bowed to its fate and let go of the vessel that had once held it. The soul tipped into the palm of his hand, and as he made contact, Death became privy to every fragment of this soul's life. From birth to death, every choice, every action, every consequence.

He relieved their last moments. For the King Consort, it was the aching struggle to pull in one final breath and the warm familiarity of home as his daughter's voice washed over him, reading aloud. Death opened a small orb that he carried on his belt, carved from the black opal found deep in the earth of Iriya. He didn't wait to see more as he tipped the soul inside. A sigh escaped him as he lost contact. The burdens of every dead man weighed too heavily on his shoulders.

He reached for the dead queen next, coaxing her reluctant soul from her body. It stubbornly resisted, clinging to the life and purpose it had once had. A feral, primal fae growl rolled from the back of his throat. A reprimand to behave and a demand to follow his will.

The soul shuddered, released.

From the corner of the room, a female gasped.

Death's head snapped up, meeting a stormy, wide-eyed gaze and with a jolt he realised that there was a second princess hiding in the corner, and she could see him.

"Fuck." Death uttered into the quiet.

It had been over twelve hundred Solisan years since he had fallen into his position and finally something surprised him.

3

At first, Keziah had thought she was dreaming and had fallen asleep where she stood. She had glanced up to find a tall and unfamiliar male leaning over her parents' bed. Strangely, Kalani did nothing to stop him. She didn't acknowledge him at all. He had pressed his hands against their unmoving chests, and with confusion Keziah watched as he coaxed a strange light from the hearts of her parents.

She slapped her hand over her mouth to stifle her gasp. Long ago, Keziah had learned to be seen and not heard, and her surprise was too noisy in the otherwise quiet bedchambers.

It wasn't quickly enough, both the male and her sister's heads turned, and she found herself pinned beneath their gazes.

While the new queen should have been the focus of her attention, Keziah couldn't look away from the male.

Her sister dismissed her quickly, turning back to her soft prayers, but the male continued to watch. He had fine and birdlike features, a narrow, pointed chin and thin lips. His eyes were soft at the corners, the colour of honeysuckle and darkened with demonic shadow.

The hair on the back of Keziah's neck stood up, an instinctive warning to look away, but she couldn't bring herself to do it. The male's long white hair that covered much one side of his face, but she could see that he cropped his hair to his scalp on one side.

His thin lips parted, as if she had startled him with her surprise. His gaze was void of emotion, and his attention had her body turning hot and cold.

Keziah trembled, unable to move thanks to her sister, and willing him not to approach. It took a moment to find her voice.

"What are you doing?" Keziah asked.

The male reeled backwards, jerking back from the bed. His fist closed tightly over the light he had stolen from the old queen's chest. He was quick to pull a sphere from his belt and hide it away.

Panic flooded Keziah's veins as it disappeared. He was a thief.

"What are you doing?!" she repeated.

"Keziah!" her sister rebuked sharply. "Who are you talking to?"

She glanced at her sister's unhappy face, and then back to the male who observed them both.

His nostrils flared. He took a quick step backwards.

"Can't you see him?!" Keziah shrieked, gesturing to the man. He stiffened wearily.

Kalani twisted. Confusion splayed across her features as she peered at the space across the bed. "See who?"

"The male!"

"There's nobody here but us, Keziah!"

"Yes, there is!" Keziah felt frantic, her head spun. "There's a male right there. Right above Papa and he's stealing their magic."

"Keziah!" her sister snapped.

"Kalani!" she cried back. "I am telling you the truth. I swear it!"

She pointed at the male, and he moved swiftly to the left, away from the ominous mark of her finger, as if he thought she might curse him.

Kalani didn't even bother to look. "Stop making things up!"

"He right there! He's leaving!" Keziah shrieked wildly as the male backed away from them. Panic flooded in her veins. "He's leaving with their magic, Kalani! Why are you pretending you can't see him?!"

A scoff of frustration rolled from her older sister, half a shriek of her own. Loud enough to call attention to them, the new queens' distress would always bring others running.

The doors bounced open. Guards rushed in, but they moved straight past the man as if he didn't exist. Keziah didn't understand why nobody else could see him. Tall and muscled, swathed in dark clothes, this male would have been hard to miss in any circumstance, let alone in a room where only royal blood should exist. Where her father had been the only male permitted.

The male moved towards the door with lithe grace, but paused there, and glanced back over his shoulder at Keziah, as if she were the curiosity out of place, and not him.

His void-like eyes narrowed on her face, and Keziah sucked in a deep breath. She called on every ounce of power she had, admittedly not much, but a drop more since her mother had died.

"*Stop!*" Her voice came out like a melody, soft and sweet. "*Stop right there, right now!*"

The guards froze in place as her magic settled across the room, a gossamer layer of compelling suggestion.

The male tilted his head, proving that he could still move where, for a breath, the guards had obeyed her desire. He assessed her, leaving Keziah feeling exposed, and those thin lips twisted up into the barest hint of a laugh before he disappeared.

There one moment and gone the next.

Kalani slapped her, a sharp smack to her cheek that pulled Keziah's attention from the male back to the moment, to the drunk feeling that had flooded through her, the ultimate high. Her sister stood tall, her umber skin glowed with power, shimmering beneath the low light.

"*Release them*." The queen's power overrode all else. Keziah's magic wilted beneath her sister's command. The magic in her veins cut short and pain ricocheted through her head so sharply that it pulled a cry from her throat. Her magic didn't hold like steel shackles the way her mother had, the way Kalani's would. It disintegrated, like sand slipping between her fingers.

The guards shifted into action the moment her magic faded. There was undeniable rage splayed across their faces as they marched forward, surrounding the new queen, and moved Kalani out of harm's way.

Keziah let out a humourless laugh. Her mother had ensured a long time ago that she couldn't harm her sister. She had not been the threat in this room.

"You could have stopped him. You could have their magic back..."

Their heads shook, Keziah glanced up and saw their pitying expressions before she let her gaze fall back down to her soft slippers. The last thing she wanted was to pity or for them to think her parents' passing had turned her soft.

Queen Kalani cleared her throat, smoothing the front of her soft skirts, and stepped forward. The new queen radiated power, her skin shined like polished bronze and her eyes showed a storm that nobody else would survive.

"*You will never speak of this again.*" The command hit Keziah like a second slap to the face. It hurt more than the first.

It was the first step her sister had taken to becoming their mother, an everlasting command that chipped away at Keziah's free will.

"*You will tell nobody these lies of stolen magic.* All their magic is mine."

Keziah bit her lip and shifted uneasily as the magic settled into place. Her lips parted as she tried in vain to tell Kalani what it had looked like, the gleaming ball of magic that had risen from Queen Kalliah's still chest, but nothing rolled of her tongue.

The magical gag was quick and effective.

Bound by another command, Keziah lost another piece of herself. Her gaze burned with fury as the new Queen straightened again, her fingers caressed against Keziah's burning cheek. Soft, regretful in the gentle movement.

It took every ounce of her remaining will for Keziah not to flinch away.

"Be good now." The new queen walked out, guards in tow, and left her sister in a room of corpses and tears.

New siren queens assumed their position the moment that their mother's power ascended to them upon death. A coronation was simple an excuse for a party rather than a formality, although each queen still held one after an appropriate period of mourning, it signified the start of a period of courting and a wave of fertility across the court, as the magic gave permission for the next generations of sirens to conceive. Queen Kalani sat proudly on her throne, revelling in her increased power within ten minutes of leaving their parents' bedchamber. Keziah realised it meant in the interim; she was an heir. Her a place in the world had changed.

It was strange for her to accept this, an unattainable and temporary position she had longed for throughout her life. It was a fraction more power, the realisation that she mattered a bit more now, even if nobody acknowledged it.

In the day that had passed, Kalani had unwittingly undone one of their mother's sung curses and allowed her sister to join the mourning ceremonies and the coronation to follow.

It was a freedom she felt inherently grateful for, even if it had come as part of an additional layer of magic controlling her mind.

"Thank you!" Keziah whispered, attempting to stifle a smile because it was a sorrowful occasion, even if this new allowance caused her heart to sing, "I haven't been to

Kalani had waved a hand dismissively.

"Just don't embarrass me, that's my rule. Carnality will be here today and Dreamous tomorrow."

She smiled softly at the queen and nodded in quick agreement; Keziah thought it would be an easy rule to follow.

The entire courts would come, and nobody would pay attention to a second princess when there was a new queen on the throne. All three siren races in one place, as it was a rare event for a siren queen to die. They thrived on their magic and lived for near on a millennium. Quaver Castle would fill to the brim, and it was easier to avoid attention in a crowd.

It offered Keziah the chance to do what she wanted without detection, especially when the other second princesses came to play.

True to the queens' prediction, Carnality was the first to arrive. They valued punctuality where their Dreamous counterparts arrived late, lost in their own thoughts.

Their courtiers flooded through the castle, easily recognisable in their daring attire. Carnality sirens had bodies envied around Solis, voluminous curves in all the right places, and the confidence to flaunt it. They strode through the halls in draped dresses of sheer fabrics, and too often Keziah caught herself staring at dusky nipples or the shadow between their plump thighs. When caught, she flushed, but the sirens preened.

Carnality sirens knew what to do with their bodies, and their magic fed on lust and desire. Their magic stoked arousal in others, and the more they fucked, the more powerful they became. Their Queen was generous in sharing her power, and much of their territory revelled in it.

The Quaver court waited in the grandest of their reception halls, Kalani sat regally on the throne and Keziah stood quietly by her side as the visitors filled in, seating themselves among the courtiers.

The final entrants, three beautiful sirens, strode into the room and approached and approached the throne.

Queen Elvira of Carnality kept no King Consort and dallied with a new male each week. Many men could have sired her daughters, although they still looked alike, destined to maintain features of their mother's royal blood.

Aubrie, the Carnality heir, stood to her right, and once her mother nodded, she swept in front of her queen and with a soft cry reached for Kalani, who rose from the throne.

They entwined, and Aubrie crushed her in a hug. The Carnality sirens adored skin to skin contact, finding reasons to touch one another in even the most mundane of situations.

Keziah felt overwhelmingly bitter at the sight of their hug and the freedom to move impulsively. Their mother had never restricted her sister, and now, as the Queen of Quaver, Kalani could still do anything she wanted.

Aubrie's younger sister caught Keziah's eye and winked, easing the dark edge of her mood.

Theodosia, who preferred the name Thea, had cut most of her dark hair off. It sat around her ears, sticking in every direction, and gave her the appearance of a mischievous pixie.

Unsurprisingly, it was an apt description for the female.

Queen Elvira took her seat in one of the ornate guest thrones to Queen Kalani's right, and they bowed their crowned heads close, exchanging brief words that offered condolences and promised further conversation.

Thea floated to Keziah's side.

"Kez, darling!" Thea greeted brightly, pressing her full lips against Keziah's mouth in a soft kiss of greeting. "I've missed you!"

Keziah blinked, caught unawares, and Thea laughed, adjusting the silver diadem across her friends' brow, soft fingers brushing her skin. It was hard to feel lonely with Thea around, and until the Dreamous Court arrived, she would bask in her friend's attention.

"I've missed you, too." She said finally.

Nobody paid them any heed, two second born princesses that lingered beside the thrones. Unimportant in the eyes of the court. Thea tangled her fingers through Keziah's and pulled her towards the door. "Let's get some air, Kez."

"What about Kalani?"

"She has things to discuss with my mother! All boring politics for your sister now." Thea announced, her voice raising in a sensual laugh. "Such are the woes of being the queen."

"Okay, okay..."

There was no time to second guess it, and they fled the castle, slipping away through the back doors.

Over the years, the three youngest children of the royal bloodlines had become close, all destined for a similar, dire fate.

They tumbled into the courtyard garden and Keziah reached to tug at a lock of Thea's short, black hair. "I like this!"

Thea giggled, her face bright with joy. "The Queen hates it! So, of course I'm keeping it! I'll never grow it out again."

"Anything to annoy your mother!"

"You know it." Thea beamed. "We second daughters need to rebel somehow."

Keziah had always been envious of the way other siren races had more freedom. They were uncontrolled by their Queens, or at least not in the way her mother had manipulated her. The same path of corruption Kalani descended.

Thea sighed, twirled, and draped herself across one of the stone benches by the pond. Her back arched, breasts pressing against the sheer crop top she wore, and Keziah fought and failed not to stare at the dark shadow of her nipples.

"Oh!" she breathed. "You've pierced them?"

Thea grinned wickedly. Her fingers tugged at the hem of her shirt and flipped it up, exposing her breasts. Her nipples pebbled in the cool air as she flaunted herself with no shame, each one threaded with a glittering bar. "You like?"

Keziah nodded. "Fuck, you're brave, Theodosia."

"They make me feel sexy." She tugged on one absently, and laid back, not bothering to cover herself back up.

"You are sexy, Thea." Keziah admitted.

In comparison, she felt unimpressive. Keziah had curves, but they didn't feel like they were in the same places, she didn't carry them with the confidence that her friend did, after so many years of being seen and not heard, fading into the background, she didn't feel the heat of desire or affection in the way others looked at her; she was nobody, and there was nobody who caught her eye either.

Thea wanted everyone, but especially Quinn, the youngest child of the Queen of the Dreamous Court and the third doomed princess.

"Do you think Quinn will like them?" Thea asked.

"Is that really a question?"

"Yes..." Thea laughed. "No."

Keziah smiled; she had known this was coming. Every time there was an excuse for the three courts to be cordial and visit one another, Thea sought ways to hold Quinn's attention; and Keziah knew even when they were apart, they remained connected.

Quinn walked through Thea's dreams nightly. It was half the reason Thea looked so tired all the time. She spent her waking and sleeping hours enjoying the pleasures of the flesh. She always carried the soft, healthy glow of renewed energy.

It often turned Keziah into a third wheel when they spent time as a group, but she ignored it, for the sake of having no other friends and not wanting to lose the few she had made.

They lay in soft silence, basking in the mid-morning sun, until Thea bolted upright. "They're here!"

"What?" Keziah quickly jumped up, and the world tilted as her head spun. "Who's here?"

"Quinn!"

"Already?"

Thea beamed. "They're early for once!"

"That's the second most surprising thing to happen all week."

Thea twisted to look back at her from where she had straightened her outfit and started for the receiving hall. "What was the first?"

"I saw a man—" Keziah began before the magic stopped her tongue, the bonds of compulsion silencing her quickly.

"A man?!" Thea's entire face brightened, eyes wide, and cheeks glowing. It wasn't often that Keziah showed interest in others. "Was he gorgeous?"

With a hum, Keziah thought of the invisible thief. He had been tall and undoubtedly stunning, but there had been something about him that left her weary.

With some retrospect, Keziah couldn't deny it.

"Yeah," she tested the words against the magic. Careful not to even hint at where she had seen him. "In a damaged way."

Thea sighed dramatically. "Beautifully broken men. How yummy." She squeezed Keziah's hand. "Do point him out when you see him tonight."

Keziah didn't have the heart, nor the resilience against the queen to voice that the male would not be at their feast, and instead nodded, pasting a soft, fake smile across her lips.

They walked back into the castle, separating at the doors and moving to stand behind their respective queens. Kalani threw her a dark look that told Keziah her the queen had noted her absence.

Queen Silene of the Dreamous Court floated through the doors ahead of her daughters, Vilianne, and Quinn. A tall woman with a firm chin and blonde hair piled on top of her head.

Their court was the most eclectic of the sirens, there was no continuity in the appearance of their royal blood, for the Dreamous picked their heirs and spares from their territory, instead of birthing them, never had a Dreamous queen borne child. They took in sirens without a drop of magic, stating if they could dream in their sleep, they would be most welcome, and that would be magic enough. Their dreams would feed their queen and that was all Queen Silene asked of her subjects, to open their minds and their fantasies for those with magic to feast.

For this reason, Vilianne was a wild red head with freckle smattered skin, and Quinn was a large female with blue-black hair to her thighs and dimples that puckered in cheeks every time she smiled.

Queen Kalani appeared stiff and unsure as they approached, but Queen Silene simply greeted her formally and took her place in one of the three thrones. Between the two aged matriarchs, Keziah's sister had never looked so small, so young and so unworthy.

The room overflowed with bodies, and attention settled on the throne. Keziah watched as Kalani tossed her dark curls over her shoulder and lifted her head proudly, as if the weight of the crown were nothing but a minor inconvenience and she could carry it for the rest of her life without fatigue.

"Welcome," Kalani spoke, her voice gentle. It wavered in pitch, but as she stood, she gained her confidence, and the soft melody of her power wove into every word. Her russet skin glowed with soft power as her song reached so many ears. "I am Queen Kalani of Quaver, and I welcome you to my court. Today, we will feast on the best that our lands offer, a tribute to the produce that thrived beneath my mother's reign. As my mother would have wanted of us, *I insist you indulge, dance, and enjoy*—"

Queen Kalani had come alive. Her magic settled over Keziah like a net, and she struggled against it instinctively, fighting to gain control of her free will. But artificial happiness flooded in her veins regardless, the struggle was futile. She was not the only one affected as magic settled across the entire room.

Queen Kalani wanted a cheerful party, and she commanded everyone except the other queens to be so, she glowed bronze as her power took hold.

Keziah wore a magic-forced grin that hid the panic she felt inside. She wanted to beg her sister to remove to magic, and let her choose what to do, choose what to feel. She wanted to beg her to reconsider using her powers to manipulate sirens that were not her own.

The words stuck in her throat, however, and she remained silent. Another of her mother's old commands that you do no questions the choices of your queen.

Her pulse fluttered as internally Keziah panicked about whether she had a single choice of her own left anymore and fell great fully into distraction as Thea and Quinn grasped for her hands and pulled her into the circle of merry dancing that had begun. Drink, dance and be merry, just as the queen had commanded.

Her friends didn't struggle against the foreign power, they beamed as if they could barely feel it, and their happiness was all their own, and dragged Keziah around and around into a circle, unseen behind the smile that wasn't her own, the smile she hated more than anything for it hide the shackles that bound her tight.

Keziah danced until her feet ached, and all the while she thought of the thief, who had looked up and finally, truly seen her, an invisible male who bore witness to a normally invisible siren.

4

The grass flattened beneath his boots as Death strode towards the crossroads in the centre of Iriya, a road that divided his territory into neat sections of punishment and privilege. Storm clouds brewed overhead, and the male snorted dismissively when they served, only to remind him of the girl who had accused him of thievery in Solis. The girl who had somehow seen him and had haunted his thoughts since, how she had managed the impossible, he didn't know.

He pressed onwards, following the black stone path until the road split in three directions. This was the place of ultimate judgement, where Death would look at a soul from beginning to end and decide their fate in the afterlife. There was nothing around except the opal laden stones and the road itself, the quiet of the stirring wind and the whisper of the shadows.

At the time of judgement, all souls were the same. There were no exceptional circumstances, whether the soul had been magical, demonic, or human, whether pauper or queen. He judged each soul equally. Death cared not for privilege and entitlement.

He took one of the opal carved spheres in his hand and balanced the weight of it, rolling it around. He waited, impatient, as two figures walked their separate paths to meet him at the junction.

Two halves of a whole, strangely identical yet nothing alike. They had been the first to greet him in this realm. Both had existed within it long before he had been born and would remain for eons beyond his own passing.

Yael, wreathed in light, watched over a field of eternal rest, where souls could go when their life cycles finished, and he did not destine them for the trials and hardships of life once more. They had built a city there, an echo of the best parts of their previous lives.

Yael was all things bright in Iriya, a crackling ball of energy that often felt out of place in the solemn realm Death had created. "Good evening, Grim."

Death bared his teeth in warning. "Don't call me that."

Yael chuckled and taunted softly, "You never told us your fae name, and you are ever so grim."

"Unnaturally grim, if you ask me," another voice clucked, deeper, rougher. It drew their attention.

The counterpart of Yael was Jael, an embodiment of darkness to balance out Yael's bright light. Both shifted between feminine and masculine forms as desired, both took their responsibilities seriously.

They had been the ones to convince him to take his position as Death, to teach him the balance of the four realms and to tell him the stories of the embodiments of death who had reigned before him. They had allowed him to redesign Iriya as it suited him.

"I am not unnaturally grim. I am Death, solemn by nature." It was an argument they had had many times. "Death is a sombre occasion."

"I think you've forgotten how to smile," Jael sniffed. "Yael, remind him, will you?"

Death rolled his eyes. "Can we get on with it?"

Jael frowned. "No. Yael isn't finished being concerned for your welfare yet."

The darker of the two flicked his fingers in his counterpart's direction, who straightened quickly.

"Yes! You seem distracted! What's going on?"

"Nothing." Death snapped too fast.

"Nothing never actually means nothing." Yael pressed in a sing-song voice. "You're answering like a distressed fae female. Don't tell me you've fallen in love."

Both light and dark laughed as he groaned, and not for the first time, a lonely male wished he could do this alone.

"I'm tired."

Yael narrowed her eyes. "You're always tired."

"Yael is right," Jael agreed.

"Yael is always right," Yael enthused.

"Don't talk about yourself in the third person," Death snapped. "It gives me a migraine."

"Ooh," Jael straightened, now pointing at the shadows that slithered across Death's pale skin. "You are upset about something."

Death grit his teeth and hissed through them. "Later."

"But…"

"I said later. We have souls to move."

Both light and darkness snapped to attention, their forms solidifying a little, the hazy shape of giant wings at their backs before they became utterly indistinct again, an ethereal presence rather than a corporal one. While they had existed for all the faces of death, at least, this was not their domain and they could not hold the concept of a solid form for long. Death ruled all in this realm, even the two oldest souls of light and dark.

They hummed in unison. "Ready."

Death prised open the opal orb and lifted the first of the shimmering souls from within. It looked like soft, floating strands of silver in the darkness of Death's realm. It shifted and rolled in his grip, but Death held tight so it could not escape.

"Queen Kalliah of the Quaver Sirens, Solis Realm." He named it. His eyelids closed, lashes pressed to his cheek, and Death watched the moments of Kalliah's life from start to finish. Curiously, he noted each flash of her daughter's half-terrified face in his mind, still caught on the thought of a strident voice and the way she had stared right at him.

His nose flared as Queen Kalliah's memories flickered through his mind, lips thinning into an unimpressed line, affronted. He listened closely to every layer of manipulation Kalliah had weaved in her life, an intricate web of tight control in all aspects.

His eyes snapped open as Death decided he had seen enough to decide what she deserved. He let go of the soul, it bobbed and then settled, the solid silver spreading into a thinner translucent outline of the body it had once held.

Death looked the soul of a queen in the eye and sneered.

"Penance. One thousand Solisan years." He decreed.

Jael stepped forward and captured the soul, shepherding it to his side without a word. His grip was unyielding, he had not lost a soul yet. Queen Kalliah's soul trembled as the darkness came close.

Death turned next to the second orb, and he released the soul within, letting it fall into its chosen shape before he named it. Names and titles were powerful concepts in Iriya, never taken for granted.

"Nevian, King Consort to Queen Kalliah of the Quaver Sirens, father to Kalani and Keziah, Solis Realm."

The soul shuddered. It seemed to tighten and curl in on itself. Afraid of death, he realised, and fought not to sneer again, drawing his lips back over bared teeth.

"I will not touch your soul, Nevian. Rest easy." Death stated. "I have seen your life entangled in the unavoidable commands of your Queen. I know that many of your choices were not your own. If her influence tainted all of your choices, then to judge your soul by those would be a disservice to who you truly are."

Death was fair, occasionally.

The soul glowed slightly, and Yael tilted her head, a soft smile twisting on her face before they faded into light again.

"He's pleased." Yael interpreted, even though Death had long since learned the languages of all the beings he collected and the ancient murmurs of souls. He did not need a translator, but Yael often took pleasure in listening to their whispers and reiterating their feelings.

"He should be." Death loathed ungrateful souls. He turned his attention back to Nevian. "I'll offer you a choice that I rarely give, King Consort."

The soul bobbed, and Death nodded slowly. He observed the soul, trusting his instincts and experience that he need not rake through Nivean's experiences and put his mind through the torture of reliving it all again.

"You may either walk with Yael to the Triplean Fields, where you may lie in eternal rest. The final path of any soul, forfeiting s chance at rebirth. Any struggles you have had will end here." He paused long enough to let it sink in. "Or you may walk the road to my right. It is a path taken alone, a road to rebirth, and another chance to live again in one of the three living realms. But I warn, the scars on your soul may be deep enough to feel in the next life over. You may have to carry the mark of what you have experienced still."

The warning was ominous, but necessary. The marks of one life could often carry through the next.

Time did not move in forward in the slow ticking of seconds within his realm, and there was no measure of how long Death stood to give this soul time to consider.

He waited in silence, gravely turning his face back to the grey skies, and giving him all the time that he needed.

Nivean shuddered before his murmured a soft word of gratefulness for the choice, something Death had seen had not been a common occurrence in his life. His queen had not been a merciful soul.

The soul bobbed, shifting out of the memory of his siren form, and without another word, floated down the long, winding path to a second chance.

"Grim," Yael cautioned, a note of sadness struck.

Death shook his head. "It is his choice alone."

Yael's light dimmed just slightly at the loss; she would have liked to see the soul choose a path of more permanent peace for all he had suffered.

Their attention turned to Jael, who poked at the soul of Queen Kalliah with tendrils of darkness, and the soul dimmed in response, coiling away.

"One thousand Solisan years repenting in the Oplean Underground, and then you'll have a chance for reconsideration."

The soul protested with an ear-splitting shriek, and Death frowned. "Speak again and I will double your time."

The darkness around Jael doubled, feeding of the shadows that licked at Death's skin, wreathing his hands like gloves, shadows that wanted to wreak havoc.

Jael dragged his new soul away.

Death barely restrained himself from letting the shadows out, fisting his hands by his sides and turning away.

"We still need to talk," Yael reminded him.

"I said later!" Death roared, agitated. He shifted through the realms before Yael could protest.

Danye was waiting. She always knew when he entered Kihnes, intuitively aware of all the comings and goings of her realm. It was necessary to ensure the worst of her demons didn't escape through thin barriers between the realms. Despite the fae heritage that should have had him yearning for Solis, Death felt at peace in Danye's realm, among the demons and the shadows.

The shadows of his own, tethered to his will, ingrained in his soul, relaxed in this realm instead of brushing agitated against his skin, begging to for him to free them. The settled until he didn't feel like he was about to explode.

Danye sauntered forward, her serpentine hair coiled atop of her head and hissed at Death. The reptilian demon queen frowned, swatting her scaled fingers at the nearest snake in light reprimand.

"Come to collect?" She asked, sharply.

Not a lot happened in Kihnes that Danye didn't know about. She accounted for the life and every death of every demon within for, and when Death came, she always greeted him like an old friend. In a way she was, Danye had marked Death on the first day of his new destiny when he had tumbled into Kihnes without permission and certainly with no concept of the severity of such trespass. He still wore the jagged pink scars across his forearm from the piercing scratch of her claws.

"No," he huffed.

Her brows rose, the snakes hissed, but she shrugged. "Follow me."

They entered a worn-out bar, modelled after a place Danye had visited in her singular foray into Zemē. It provided a neutral space before visitors truly stepped into the horrors of the demon world, where there were few rules and only the strongest survived.

A neon pink sign blinked in and out of power above the bar that stated, 'do fun shit' and while the bar itself never had patrons, the gorgon kept it stocked with her favourites.

Danye met every visitor here, seated by the bar, poured a drink, and decided if she would allow them in or simply kill them. Often it turned out to be the latter, but beyond his first and unscheduled foray into this realm, Danye had not attacked him. Yet.

Death had collected many souls from this floor, especially when humans walked through the thinned barriers between realms on the nights where the moon hung full across all of existence, or the stars aligned in fortuitous patterns. To die at the gorgon's hand, in a bar that reminded of them of humanity, was a blessing compared to the horrors they would face if left to enter the void of the demons.

The serpentine queen reached over the bar and snagged a bottle, holding it up for his appraisal.

"Human vintage, apparently." She hissed. Death offered a thin-lipped smile.

It splashed in the base of two glasses, an amber liquid, and he gulped it down. Three glasses later and it barely hit the spot.

"Humansss are weak," Danye sniffed, and swapped it for a bottle of fae wine, the ochre label on the front familiar to the man. "Thisss stuff is complete shit."

"Humans lost their magic," Death scoffed. "Give them a break."

Danye blinked, lifted the wine bottle to her scaled lips, and took a long swig. She reached out; a scaled hand laid against his chest as if taunting him with the contact. Danye was one of the few permitted touching him.

"Why are you here?"

"Can't I visit a friend?" Death took the bottle, and the brew burned down his throat.

"Oh," Danye chuckled, amber gaze brightening. "You want to fuck. Typical male."

Death smirked. "I'm never opposed to sliding between your legs, Danye, but I wanted to discuss something else."

Kicking one leg over the other and leaning back against the bar, Danye sighed. "Fine conversation first. We both know you never stay to chat shit when the deed is done."

The eyes of every snake growing from her scalp seemed to roll as one. Death had the feeling that the Demon Queen considered this his fatal flaw. His apathy towards cuddling.

"Why can demons see me?"

Danye frowned. "Did one of my demons get in your way?"

"No," Death refuted. "A girl. A siren. She saw me. Is there a chance she could be demon blessed?"

This rattled Danye. Her snakes coiled as if to strike and her forked tongue flicked at the air, tasting it.

"Demons don't see you," she corrected, reaching between them both to pop the button on Death's pants. "They see your shadows."

"Hmm?" He prompted as her wrist snaked fluidly beneath his waistband. She closed the gap between them, her palm sliding along the length of him, and he hardened at her touch. Her snakes uncoiled, reaching for him, their flickering tongues brushing against his neck as Danye's mouth brushed against his collarbone. Her fangs scraped against a sensitive spot before she clarified.

"Demons see the shadowed outline of death, not death himself."

He pulled back, frowning.

Danye sighed. She unhooked the clasp on her tight pants and wriggled them over the curve of her arse. He couldn't help but watch as she exposed herself.

"You mean you can't see me?" He asked.

She scoffed, hoisting herself onto the bar and spreading her naked legs, unabashedly on display. "Of course, I can see you, Death. I am the demon queen, and because you will it to be so. Now—"

Danye grasped his collar and pulled him between her splayed legs. They shared a kiss, bruising lingering, and Danye growled a feral hiss from the back of her throat, her fingers winding in his white hair, claws raking gently across his scalp.

"—Drop to your knees, Death, and show me how you thankful you are..."

Death chuckled against her skin, his fingers digging into her thighs as he forced them wider. His mouth trailed a path down her chest, nipping and bite her hard nipples until she rewarded him with a hiss of pleasure. Death dropped to his knees as requested, holding her legs wide, and pressed his mouth to her core, his tongue sliding through her slick arousal, lapping at her like a male starved. He didn't stop until her head hung back, hips bucking, her serpentine hair hissing with pleasure.

He reached into his pants, fisting his cock, and stroking it from base to tip in time with the languid swipe of his tongue. "Mmm," he drew back, languidly licking his lips. "You taste far fucking better than fae wine."

When she growled in desperate demand again, her hips arching in silent request for more Death grinned a feral smile. He slid a finger into the demon queen's soaked, throbbing core, and stroked her from the inside out. A second finger joined the first, her legs spreading wider as Death dipped his head and lapped at her clit. He sucked hard while the demon queen bucked her hips, riding his fingers.

Needy pants rolled from the back of her throat, intermingled with a hissing wine, she rolled her hips, and he sank his fingers deeper inside of the demoness in reward for the pliant way she responded to him. "Good girl."

She groaned in soft pleasure, hips moving faster, claws slicing into his skin as she held him tight, barring him from moving away.

"That's it, come undone for me." Death whispered against her skin, and she writhed. His fingers plunged deeper, faster as Danye's legs tensed and trembled, and she coiled on the edge. Sharp nails pierced through his shirt, slicing against his skin as she lifted herself off the bar and ground herself against his face, taut on the edge of her pleasure.

"More," Danye demanded. "Give me more!"

Death stroked himself faster, pumping the length of his cock as Danye screamed through her orgasm, her thick thighs wrapping around his head, hips bucking until she calmed, turning liquid beneath him, panting against the bar.

Death grunted, biting her thigh hard to stifle the sounds of his pleasure, coating his own hand. He slid his fingers free of her and took a moment to lick her slick pleasure from them. His other hand he wiped on his shirt.

The demon queen, smirked lazily up at him, shifting to sit on the bar. One leg crossed over the other again, closing off his access, a thin sheen of sweat covering her scaled body. She reached for the discarded bottle of fae wine and gulped it down.

"Until next time," Danye murmured.

Death licked his lips again, tucked himself away, and didn't bother to re-button his pants. "Next time, you're on your knees."

He was still smirking when he arrived back in Iriya. He could make even a queen come apart, just as he did everyone else.

5

The forced festivities rolled from night to morning. By the time Queen Kalani realised that the night only ended when she said the word, exhaustion had set in across all three races. Especially among the Dreamous sirens, who thrived in the twilight hours when the world slept and struggled as the castle danced those hours away, deprived of the dreams they needed to restore themselves. Queen Kalani yawned and lazily lifted her influence over the castle before she disappeared to bed, her ruby red slippers scuffed along the floor as she went, the room waiting for her to disappear before they moved. She was entirely unaffected and unbothered by the struggles of everyone else, many of whom sagged to the floor and passed right out.

In the middle of the hall, Keziah sank to her knees. Her thighs trembled from dancing so much, her feet ached, and her head spun. Slowly, she peeled once comfortable gold slippers from her feet and tossed them aside.

As weary sirens fled the hall, she found the privacy to cry. It started as soft sniffles, and gave way to a floor of waterworks, salty tears that streamed down her face and left her with a bigger headache.

"Princess?" one guard cleared his throat.

Keziah looked up, swiping the back of her hand against her snotty nose. He was strangely familiar, usually standing close to Kalani. She frowned at him.

"You should get some sleep." He suggested.

She nodded, confused, since the guards usually paid her little attention. Keziah waited for him to leave, but the guard remained in place, patient and expectant.

"Princess," He cleared his throat again. "You're the heir, now. It would be my pleasure to escort you."

"Oh."

The guard nodded and held out a hand. "We'll escort you to your chambers now."

Keziah took his strong hand, and he hoisted her to her feet. She stooped to grasp the discarded slippers and turned to follow. "What's your name?"

"I am Chirit, Princess, the guard of the heir." He fell into step with Keziah before he added in gently. "My son will be approaching for your sister's hand."

"Ah," Keziah's tone lifted with surprise. "So soon."

"It is better for a new queen to birth the next generation quickly," Chirit said. "I expect many will approach."

Keziah flinched because the birth of the next generation meant the end of her life.

"I suppose it is," she breathed, and had never been more grateful to see her door. "Goodnight!"

She closed it quickly, flicked the lock and sagged to the ground, fresh tears brimming in her eyes. Death wouldn't be the worst alternative to constantly moving as a puppet, the end of the pretty ribbons secured by a selfish queen. She was tired of being a marionette.

Keziah pulled the pins from her hair, massaging her scalp, and sat with her back to the door. Exhaustion ached in every muscle, and the persistent headache cracked against her skull. Keziah fell asleep with her back to the door, on the fleeting thought that the world might be better off if she didn't wake again.

Quinn visited her dreams, tugging Theodosia along as they stumbled into a familiar field and collapsed on the grass, relaxing among the soft white dandelions. There they watched the shapes in the clouds. Such was the joy of having a siren walk through your dreams. Quinn could manipulate anything within the dreamscape and feed off the emotions it created. They could experience anything they wanted in the night, without the courts to deal with.

Normally, she specialised in nightmares. Fear was potent and delectable to the Dreamous court, and Quinn often said she preferred any scene with a chase. Keziah was grateful, though, that her friend rarely brought these elements when she visited her. She stared up at the fake sun, squinting and wishing it would dim just a touch.

"How often does your sister do that?" Quinn asked quietly.

"Do what?" Keziah yawned.

"Bend everyone to her will..."

She bolted upright, drawing her knees to her chest as her heart pounded with alarm. "You could tell?"

Quinn nodded. "We all know what you can do; our queens warn us about it before we see you. Queen Kalliah was subtle, careful, but Kalani feels like a punch to the face."

Keziah twisted the hem of her skirts between her fingers, fretting. "It's..."

Even in her dreams, the magic shackles prevented her from speaking ill of her sister, and the siren closed her eyes, pushing out a slow breath. "She's just got a lot of new power. She's learning."

Quinn scoffed. "Mama was *horrified*! At least Queen Kalliah had the respect not to affect the heirs."

Keziah said nothing.

Out of all the second Princesses, Quinn had the most respect for the hierarchical systems of heirs and spares, hand selected for her place in the world and without it, she would have been a girl without a drop of bequeathed power, destined to provide dreams for her court's survival. For Quinn, her position was a gift and not a burden.

"That's enough!" Thea cried suddenly. She sat up, wrapping an arm around Keziah's shoulders and pulling her back down to the grass. "Let's talk of nicer, sexier things."

Quinn giggled and rolled snugly into Thea's other side. "Like what?"

"Keziah met a male," Thea said brightly.

"What?!" Quinn cried, joining in Thea's bright exuberance. "And you let me talk of power politics, instead?!"

Both princesses rolled against her, and even though it was just a dream Keziah could have sworn she could feel their comforting heavy weight pressed against her, the stifling heat of their bodies. It was almost relaxing.

"Tell me again," Thea demanded.

"There's really not much to tell." Keziah hesitated.

"Did you speak to him?" Thea pressed.

Keziah shifted, "Yes, sort of... He was..."

The words stuck in the back of her throat, tears welling at the corner of her eyes. She couldn't speak of him, and it frustrated her more than anything, but because she wanted to praise his looks or whisper about the mystery of him, but because she wanted to be able to warn of the thief in the night, he who stole magic.

Quinn let out a sympathetic click of her tongue. "Did you say something silly? I'm sure he won't remember it, you're a Princess of Quaver, males will forgive us anything."

"So will females," Thea added, smirking widely.

"It's not that. It's that he was..." Frustration rolled through her, a growl rolling from the back of her throat.

Quinn propped herself up on one arm. "Come on, don't hold out on us. Start with what he looked like!"

"He's tall," Keziah was surprised she could say as much. "Taller than any male I've ever seen before."

"He's got muscles, right?" Thea giggled. "Tell me he has muscles!"

"Mhmn," Keziah agreed, thinking back to when she had seen him, two days prior. Not that he had been far from her mind since. "He wore all black, and that made him look ghostly. He was pale in the way you are, Thea."

"You mean he might be Carnality?" Both the princesses perked up at this idea.

"No," Keziah shook her head, thrilled that she could describe him, even if she couldn't warn them. "He doesn't look siren. He was... Too slender? Even under all the muscle? Too still. I don't know... He had eyes like..."

"The cerulean sea?" Quinn suggested.

Thea chimed in next, "The first drop of sunrise?"

"Oh!" Quinn gasped. "Maybe he's Mer."

"I've never had a Mer male," Thea enthused, nodding. "Apparently they have *very* skilled tongues."

A surprised squeak caught in the back of Keziah's throat, flash flushing. "But he didn't have a tail!"

Thea waved her hand imperiously. "Mer males lose their tails when they venture onto land. They'd be all strong, perfect long legs, what I wouldn't give to spend the night with one—"

"His eyes looked like the end of the world," Keziah interrupted. "They were a darkness you could get lost in."

Thea and Quinn visibly deflated, they collapsed into each other, winding their arms around each other.

Keziah felt the acute chill of feeling left out.

"Well, that's depressing," Thea murmured, and she shrugged unsure how to fix the broken conversation.

"What did he say to you?" Quinn asked a beat later.

Keziah's eyes narrowed; she had always been too perceptive for her own good. A side-effect of walking through the psyche of others.

"You obviously can't stop thinking about him if you've whittled his eye colour down to that."

Keziah sighed heavily. They were back to things she couldn't talk about, but her answer was surprisingly truthful. "Nothing."

"Nothing?" Quinn echoed.

"Nothing at all."

6

Death cringed as he slipped into Zemē and the blare of loud, city noises assaulted his ears. It was always so busy and loud. The clamour of technology was stark, compared to the gentle quiet of magic, and the humans left their mark on the four realms with the noise they created, screaming for attention. He had arrived amid a city, and somewhere to his left a crossing warbled with the alarm that the humans could pass without getting squashed by a car. It reminded him of his first foray here, when a car had almost run him down, a mistake repeated too often in the early days of this position. Time crawled here. While thousands of years had passed in Solis and Iriya, it had been barely sixty years in this realm, and still he collected so many souls. Since then, he had learned a lot about humans, their language, their eccentricities, and the technology that powered them.

Death stood still for the first few minutes. He watched they milled around him, soaking them in.

He was unseen, just as he always had been. Over the years, he learned the tongues of human, the different languages, the oldest of them now beginning to die out. Set to suffer in forgotten peril, which was the way of humans, just as they had forgotten the wonder of magic, they would lose their own ancient customs in their preoccupation with evolving further.

A sickness had come to this realm, however, near two human years ago, and ravaged through the population. Death had visited more often than usual as time spanned on.

Humans died every day, but this disease ravaged them and took more souls before their time should have come.

Even now, he arrived on a day where the death in this world reached a toll of thousands. Bodies ravaged by the virus, their organs left failing, and their prayers unheard. Nobody ever prayed to Death, but whomever they whispered to passed them into his hands all the same.

In the wake of this illness, souls lingered alone in their last moments, as he couldn't be with them throughout their final breaths. He could spend all his time in this realm and always have another to collect, or find some that had slipped through the cracks, left behind untethered on the earth.

He could not visit them all. In their last moments, he did not cleave life from a body, like the humans suspected, but visited in the moments thereafter, when life had vacated, and soul did not know what to do next. He gave them guidance and carried them towards a chance to start again.

He stretched. Death rolled up his sleeves, revealing his pale, scarred forearms. The reminder of a young male with foolish ambition to come into his own, they were an unsightly representation of how he felt on the outside.

There was a small building tucked into the outskirts of the city, where the humans placed their elderly as they waited for them to die — and many of them did. That was his first intended stop, to relieve those who had lived and suffered too long already first.

In the distance, tires squealed loudly.

Screams echoed in the shell of his ear, easily distinguished by his advanced fae hearing. Metal crunched against metal, and the pleas cut to quiet. The soft, eerie quiet of tragedy that called him forward.

Death sighed.

He turned and walked towards the mangled mess of crushed metal and shattered glass. For all his years in his position he still could not stop himself from judging the choice to hurtle around space at breakneck speed, encased in metal. He advanced on the wreckage and peered within. A woman hung upside down, caught in the restraint of her seatbelt, covered in fragments of the windshield.

Her eyelids fluttered.

"Shhh," Death willed himself to be visible to the woman. "Easy now."

As she roused to consciousness, her eyes widened, frantic and where her lips parted, no sound came out. He could tell the glamour that kept him protected had lifted because of the wild and instinctive fear in the human woman's gaze.

"Shh now," he hushed her again

When she caught his eye, the woman automatically flinched from the hue of his gaze and the shadows that rolled across his irises.

Death sighed; he reached forward. A cry rolled from her chest as she tried to avoid him, but he pressed cool fingers to her forehead, and commanded, "sleep now."

The woman's body went limp, long lashes pressing against her cheeks. Death's finger brushed against her pulse, not that he wouldn't have known when she passed, and her soul loosened, but the thrum of blood in her veins was strong enough that he thought she might survive extraction from the mess of metal and glass. If she was lucky, and if help came quickly.

Death paused, listening intently for the ear-splitting wail of sirens usually accompanied an emergency in this realm, heard from blocks away, but the noisy city did not wail with the cry of saviours, which meant they would be too far away for this woman.

He growled, unhappy, and twisted back into the wreckage. He worked at the clasp of her seatbelt, grunting when her weight fell from the roof and with effort, the male pulled her free of the wreckage.

Death lay her on the ground. She was young, he realised, although he had no true concept of human age. He guessed her to be in the middle of childhood and senility.

Her bloodied hair fanned around her head, a halo of gore. Her chest rose and fell with even movements. She slept as commanded.

Death turned his back on her and willed himself back into the shadows and the safety of obscurity. He couched at the opening of the metal carnage again, looking to the seat beyond the woman.

"You're who I want..." He murmured, speaking to the too-still passenger with a shard of metal punctured through his neck. "Come here."

He reached not for the body but for the translucent, silver-white light of the lost soul. The fear of the human's last moments slammed into him, along with the quick end to his life.

Death felt the fragments of horror. Listening to the sound of the driver's scream, he saw the world spin as the car rolled and then nothing. A flash of pain at his neck, the strange sensation of warm blood trickling down his chest and then... nothing.

The scene left him anxious, as violent deaths did, but Death cradled the soul carefully until he found a name. Then he slipped it inside the opal orb from his belt.

He always noted their names, every soul he sought, each one deserved at least a recognition of who they had been, and who they would never be again.

His nostrils flared, sniffing at the smell of deterioration and decay that had permeated through this world for some time now the rot that came with an illness their technology struggled to beat. He crawled from the wreckage and dusted shards of glass from his pants. Their bodies remained where he left them, waiting in silence, but Death did not have time for the blood and flesh vessels of souls.

He had many more names to collect in Zemē that night

7

Every three months there came a celebrated time by Sirens throughout Solis. It was a night where the moon hung bright and full across the four fabled realms and the walls between the realms grew thin, allowing passage from one to another. On these nights, many humans wandered into a world of magic, lost after turning around a corner that led them too far from home. The Sirens went hunting for prey to bring back, filling their castles with people they could manipulate, fuck, or torment through their nightmares, humans who were more susceptible to their magic and keeping them powerful and satiated.

Keziah was giddy with child-like excitement; it left her fluttering through the halls. Under her mother's reign, she had dared not ask if she could attend the celebrations, join the hunting parties, and make use of the way her power doubled under this heavy moon. Her mother had always forbidden her daughters to venture into another realm, instructing others to bring their prey back.

Her strength of will, her dandelion spine, had not been strong enough to brave the wrath and restriction that may have come if she had suggested it to Queen Kalliah.

The new queen was different. Kalani had waved off the request as if it had never been a question. Keziah hadn't had to grovel or plea, because her sister was more irritated with the interruption to her time than anything else. Queen Kalani had an upcoming coronation to plan and between that and the suitors that vied for her attention, she had little time for anything else.

While the sun dipped below the horizon, Keziah prepared herself, pinning half her thick curls up, rimming her eyes in black and gold, painting her dark skin with oils and powders that left it shimmering akin to the way her skin brightened with the use of her magic.

When she stepped back from the mirror, soft skirts flared around her even softer hips and swaying around her ankles, the cropped off the shoulder Quaven style of top left her soft stomach bared. Tiny bells tinkling at her wrists. She looked alive, healthier than she had in months. At the last moment, after hesitating too long, she removed the gold diadem that usually sat on her brow, an indicator of royal blood, and placed it gently on her pillow. She wanted to be just like everyone else for one night.

Nothing could steal the smile from her face, not even the trickle of insecurity that she was not enough for this, that she would never look as good as her sister. A call from the hall drew her away, and Keziah followed it, before she could second guess herself and reach for the diadem and the safety of home again.

In the main reception hall, Quavers, Carnality and Dreamous alike swanned around in their best outfits, indulging in treats, and waiting for the sun to sink full beneath the horizon.

Thea wore a short dress that barely covered her arse, her long legs on display, her full lips painted the colour of the succulent inside of a black cherry. She was enticing, her eyes hooded with sexual energy, and her smile a promise of fun.

Quinn had turned into an embodiment of the dark and starry night. She danced alongside Thea, her hair pin straight, her eyes rimmed dark hair straight as a pin. Every sway of her hips caused her dress to inch higher up her thick thighs and it glittered like stars at midnight.

Queen Kalani rose languidly from her throne and a hush settled across the room. Keziah gazed up at her sister, arms folding across her stomach as she realised. She, in fact, paled compared to Kalani's slender beauty and the refinement of the way her curls pinned around her glittering crown.

Insecurity was a fickle beast, and her eyes dropped to her feet, unable to watch through the announcements.

"The High Moon has come," Kalani announced. "Tonight, you may enter the realm of men and women. You bring magic to a world where it does not remain and, in return, a gift for the heathen race. I ask that you bring back gifts for us, all an offering from the humans."

She lifted in her chin; her dark lashes fluttered. The young Queen smiled widely at her court and their guests. "Bring us the human sacrifices. Bring us their minds to play with, their dreams to possess, bring us their hunger for pleasures of the flesh."

Kalani stepped forward down the steps of the dais until she stood, shoulder to shoulder, with her court. "We are Sirens, and under the high moon, we are unstoppable."

A cheer rose from all three courts, loud and lifting, until Keziah couldn't stop herself from peeking at the room again, the corner of her mouth twitching into a soft smile.

The High Moon was time for hunting and pleasure, a time where Sirens became drunk on their own power. It was no place for her self-doubt. She needed to pull herself together.

"Come on!" Thea cried, threading her fingers through Keziah's, and holding tight. She reached for Quinn, too. "Let's wait at the Starbright Pools."

The Starbright Pools were a portal from Siren territory to the dark depths of the Mer Sea, where dark Mer rose from the depths to supply jestweed above ground, although officially it was for when politics required the two species to conduct business. It was here that the three Siren Queens would meet with the King of the Saltwater Mer, or any of his seven princes. Young sirens often stood at the edge, tried to peer through the depths of the water as if they might glimpse a scaled tail, or the fabled city far below. All Keziah had ever seen was darkness.

Some, confident with middle life, tried to dive in, and swim as deep as they could try to reach the city, on the rumour that only the strong of heart could make it, and only those made it would receive the reward of breath beneath water. Of course, they all came back gasping for air and proclaiming that it was too dark down there to see anything.

Once, when Keziah was much younger, and still close to Kalani, her sister sung a song to one nobleman's son who had taken to following her around.

With soft dulcet tones, she ordered him to dive into the into the glittering waters. She sang the song of a boy who swam down to the Mer city. He swam and swam, never returning for air. He swam until he found the single Mer princess and, with her kiss, received precious air again.

The nobleman's son's eyes had glazed over, a dreamy smile of compliance pulling at his lips. He tore off his shirt, much to Kalani's delight, and dove into the water without hesitation. There was never any choice when the magic of a

Quaver song set in. Just the utter compulsion to do as commanded.

Keziah fret by her sister's side as he stayed below the dark depths. Unseen. Seconds ticked into minutes. She knew how he must have felt in the moments before he dived back, the small part of him that must have been panicking, screaming for the freedom to resist.

"Call him back!" Keziah demanded, but Kalani simply laughed and shook her head.

"He'll come back when he finds the Mer City."

Keziah paled. "It's just a story, Kala. We can't reach the Mer city. He can't breathe down there. He'll die."

"Well," Kalani scoffed, suddenly so alike in their mother that Keziah flinched. "He shouldn't have been so annoying, then."

Less than a day later, his dead body floated back to the surface of the pools, bloated with water, scratched, and bitten by the sea creatures below.

Since then, Keziah had vowed never to enter the glittering pools. Even on the High Moon, when her power felt like it hummed beneath her skin, she sat back on the soft grass and watched wearily as Thea and Quinn discarded their shoes and dipped their legs into the pools. With time, others joined siren men and woman dressed to celebrate, and they laughed and giggled as the moon slipped higher and higher into the sky.

When the moon reached its peak, the eldest of the Siren's stood and nodded. She was one of Carnalities' best huntresses. "It's time."

Keziah stood. Her heart raced in her chest as she reached for Thea's hand to anchor herself. Her friends had been to Zemē before, but it was all an unfamiliar experience for Keziah, who dreaded it as much as she desired it.

What if she became lost and could never come home? What scared her most, though, was that not coming back didn't sound like the worst option of all.

At the entrance to a shallow cave, just beyond the pools, the air seemed to shimmer as the veils between the realms shifted. It was here that sirens of all three courts converged. They stepped forward, through the veil, and disappeared and the passage would remain open for as long as the moon remained in the sky.

Keziah was slow to approach. Nervousness left the bells at her wrists tinkling gently. She waited on the precipice of one world and the next, hesitating until Quinn let out a laugh and, with a hard shove, pushed her right through.

The human world was dull compared to the colours and life of Solis, shrouded in darkness created by the towering, solid buildings in varying shades of grey. Glass and metal that loomed above everything. The sirens spilled out of the woods and into a clearing strung with tiny, glittering lights. They laughed and cheered, dancing in circles and as they came across humans, sirens peeled away from the group to capture their attention.

Quinn took Keziah by the hand. She reached for Thea and together they separated from the group, turning out of the park and into the streets. They ran down the empty roads, beneath the full light of the High Moon.

The strange wonder and the lingering cold of this world left her amazed, and Keziah slowed her friends down as she tried to drink everything in.

"Come on!" Quinn bossed.

"But—" Keziah had paused, staring at a bicycle tried to a pole. It didn't move the more she watched it, but they had tied to the pole like a misbehaving pet. She didn't understand it.

"Come on, we need to find humans," Quinn tugged her forward and Keziah stumbled after her, twisting for one glance back at the peculiar sight.

"Do they tie it up so it doesn't run away or because it's dangerous?" She asked.

Thea just laughed. "Who knows! The humans are a strange race."

Keziah's blood seemed to sizzle in her veins, filled with an energy that lit her up from the inside out. They walked through the darkness until they spotted a stray human. Her head ducked low, the tassels on her dress swinging with every teetering step she took down the path. She stood on slippers with a tall point at the heel, which looked more like a torture device than anything else Keziah had seen so far.

Quinn nudged Keziah with a whisper. "Call her over. Sing, Kez!"

Keziah flinched; nervousness fluttered in her belly.

The few times she had used her power in childhood had been accidental, flared beneath the same luminescent moon that guided them now. Her shoulders rolled back, spine straightening, her hands fluttering at her midsection as Keziah cleared her throat.

Dark lashes pressed against her full cheeks; Keziah inhaled deeply. She reached for the thread of power curled within her soul.

"*Hey, you,*" she called, and the words rolled off the end of her tongue in the soft, ancient language of the sirens, unfamiliar to a human but pretty enough to capture their attention. They twisted with a soft melody that rose and fell from the end of her tongue. "*Come over here.*"

The human turned, pushing blonde strands of hair from her face, a frown twisted on her lips. "What did you say?"

Thea rocked onto the balls of her feet, an excited smile twisted across her face, flashing perfect white teeth. The glimmer in her eyes looked predatory.

"Speak English," Quinn reminded them all breathlessly. Keziah inhaled sharply and drew another breath. As a Princess of Quaver, she had learned the language of their favoured prey, but it took a moment to find the right movement for her tongue, the right lilt of the syllables. The common human tongue always felt strange in her mouth, the vowels blunt. It was harder to infuse power into their words.

"*Come over here, come and play with us...*" Keziah sang. Her voice was softer than her sisters, a husky gentle coax instead of a belted, undeniable command. Manipulation instead of force.

Still, it worked.

The human's eyes glazed over, and she swayed on the spot, teetering back towards them on her dangerous heels, her compliance fed through Keziah like a drug.

Her head spun, her lungs expanded, and she felt as if she had never taken a full, pure breath of air before this moment. Her skin shimmered bronzing her already dark umber undertones, energy pushed outwards, as she fed on the compliance.

She wanted more.

The human girl hesitated, confusion crumpled across her brow, as if she couldn't remember what she was doing a moment ago, or how she got to be here. It reminded Keziah quickly that without weaving timelines and permanency into her commands, magic was fleeting, black sand slipping through her fingertips, suggestion lost in the intricacies of her mind.

Thea stepped in smoothly, her arm wrapped around the human's shoulders, and the Carnality Princess pulled the girl in to embrace as if they were long-lost friends. Their bodies moulded together, Thea's fingertips brushing down the blonde woman's spine and stirring feelings that fed the siren's desire for contact in intimacy. She drew back and kissed the human on the lips, her pale skin taking on a soft glow of power.

"It's so good to see you," Thea murmured.

The girl smiled softly, but the furrow of her brows didn't shift, and she blinked rapidly as if trying to clear the overwhelming fog from her senses.

"*What's your name?*" It came easier now for Keziah to sing the syllables instead of simply speaking.

With every passing moment, she wanted nothing more than to do it again. "*You're safe here. We are old friends... you feel you've known us forever... You will always relax with us.*"

Unthinkingly, Keziah did what she had once sworn she would never do and settled a permanent command across someone else's free will. The effects were like nothing else. Her heart raced, her body throbbed with pleasure, and her blood felt light. She knew she should have felt guilty, but the wash of her amplifying power was addictive, a giddying high far better than any Mer drug.

The human visibly relaxed.

Keziah of Quaver smiled widely, and she had never looked so alive. Her sea-storm eyes were a bright and wild grey, delight clear in her features.

"I'm Tahnee," the human whispered. Tahnee shook her head and sunk into the magically forced familiarity, accepting the call of the song. "I've missed you all."

Quinn leaned in and took Tahnee's other hand, sandwiching the human between the two of them, and smiling down at her. "We've missed you too! It feels like we've been waiting a lifetime for you."

Three months between hunts, three months during which the supply of humans in Solis dwindled, could feel like a lifetime, indeed.

"Where were you going, Tahnee?" Quinn asked. The question didn't need a magical edge, but still Keziah felt disappointment, a seed of resentment planted in the pit of her stomach.

She waited for the answer, giving Quinn her moment.

"Todd's party!" Tahnee chirped.

"Oh! Quinn grinned. "May we come with you?"

Tahnee, embed by the magic that assured the three sirens were the best of her friends, didn't hesitate to grin and nod. "Of course! Follow me!"

They twisted, and Thea let go as the Quinn and the human led the way. She dropped back to where Keziah stood, and the two of them basked in power.

"You're gorgeous, Kez." Thea whispered, her thumb dragging over Keziah's full lower lip, the simple touch sending energy to Thea, too. "You look like fae-coffee stirred with liquid gold."

"Thea..." Even flooded with power, knowing that she was radiant, Keziah struggled with the compliment.

Thea shook her head. "I'm telling the truth, Keziah. Look at yourself. You are irresistible, just as we sirens should be."

She did, her gaze dropping to the soft shimmer of her skin, the shades of colour in her wild curls, which usually appeared so dull in the mirror.

"Won't the human's notice?" She giggled nervously, reaching the extent of her flexibility in her confidence, and folding back on herself.

She looked to where Quinn engaged the human. Quinn, who had not fed and seemed to look sickly compared to the life within them.

Thea shook her head; she took Keziah's hand and tugged her along so they could catch up.

"Humans are fantastic at just explaining things away. It might be their greatest skill." Thea advised and grinned wickedly. "Even if we danced, glowing, magical and buck naked in front of them. Which, you know, I still might do tonight."

They hurried to follow Tahnee, coming to a tall rise building and passing through the glass doors and into a metal box. The doors slid closed, securing them in, and Keziah's hand curled around the metal bar that lined the edges, suddenly feeling cooped up.

Tahnee seemed undisturbed. She consulted a strange, slim rectangle that glowed back up at her and then stabbed at a button on the side of the wall.

It too lit up, and when the metal box shuddered and rose, Keziah felt like her stomach was falling out. Her knuckles blanched; full lips pressed together tightly.

A nervous giggle rose from her lips, and she slapped her palm across her mouth to stifle it.

Thea and Quinn grinned back.

Keziah realised this must not be so new to them. They hunted and brought back prey of their own to sustain them. Thea found a new body to curl around in bed, feeding with each moment of contact. Even now, she dragged her fingers up and down Tahnee's arm, working her magic as Tahnee leaned into her touch. Whereas Quinn searched for an intriguing or broken mind, a place where dreams would be interesting and fractured, where she could spin a story, and created an influence that would keep her healthy and fed.

Keziah didn't know what she wanted from this hunting expedition, and the question haunted her long after the metal doors slid open and revealed the rooftop party.

It was different to the way sirens celebrated, and not at all what she had expected. The humans didn't dress too grandly; they didn't dance but mingled into little clusters. Drinks in hand, faces too close, laughter loud in the air.

There were chairs that sat forgotten, and old sofas that carried bodies tangled within one another. Humans twisted around each other, desperate for contact.

Thea lit up at the sight of them.

"Love you and leave you..." she called to Keziah and Quinn, drifting to the couples to find her place to join.

Keziah's nerves frayed slightly, a mixture of excitement and fear sparking in her veins, and she turned to Quinn only to realise the other siren had disappeared too, seamlessly joining a pocket of conversation and she was on her own.

Always alone, the little princess with the soft, destroyable spine. Even in the throes of power, self-doubt was a poison, and Keziah swallowed, her mouth suddenly dry.

Tahnee came to her rescue, pushing strands of her heavy blonde fringe from her eyes and reaching for Keziah's arm. "Come on, let me introduce you..."

Before she knew it, Keziah was standing at the edge of the rooftop, pressed against cold stone, covered in vine, while Tahnee called out the names of an array of unfamiliar faces.

"—and this is..." Tahnee frowned. Her body shivered as the magic reminded her they were old friends, but her mind revolted against the obvious gap in information. Old friends, but she didn't know her name, a rookie error.

"Kez..." the siren offered.

Tahnee's face lit up with a soft red blush. She tossed her head back and laughed nervously. "I'm so, *so* sorry. I completely forgot your name! I'm the worst friend, a teensie bit of tequila, and I'm gone."

Keziah shook her head. "It's fine."

"It's really not," Tahnee passed over the small glass in her hand and brushed her fringe off her forehead again. "Take this one off me before I'm too smashed to function. I'll go find water."

The little glass was cold beneath her fingertips. Keziah inspected the clear liquid in it. When she looked up, Tahnee's other friends were watching her closely.

"Go on..." One said, a man with brown hair that stuck in all directions.

"What?" Keziah spluttered.

"Drink it," He encouraged.

"I'm just holding it until..."

"You'll be double parked when she comes back if you don't drink it quick," someone else laughed. "Tahnee's going for more tequila, not water. She never drinks water."

"I don't know..." In all her lessons about Zemē, taught by a severe Quaver Siren gifted with just enough power to ensure the information stayed with them, and had instructed three generations of royal blood, she had never heard of those words: double parked.

"Oh!" A woman brightened with understanding. "Guys, she's from like..." Her voice dropped to a whisper. "*Another country.* Stop using slang."

"Uhh," Keziah chewed on her bottom lip. She looked for the safety of Thea and Quinn, but they were too preoccupied to catch her gaze. Thea seemed to glow like a new moon, but nobody noticed, too wrapped up in their own moments.

Someone nudged her, and Keziah slammed back to the conversation at hand.

"It means you'll be holding two drinks, which is against the rules..."

Keziah hadn't known there were rules to drinking, there were no rules at home.

Tahnee reappeared. She pushed a second small glass into Keziah's other hand and true to the human's predictions, she and Tahnee were now 'double parked.'

The circle of friends let out a laugh, and as one, they all sang:

"Here's to Tahnee, she's true blue. She's a piss pot through and through. She's a bastard, so they say, and she's not going to heaven, so she went the other way. She's going down, down, down, down!"

Tahnee grinned wildly throughout the entire song, and on the second last down, she lifted the tiny glass and drained it dry in one swallow. Keziah didn't know what they were singing about, but she was amazed that their song had worked, even without magic, and even though they all sounded awful as they sang.

The collective attention of the small circle turned back to her, and the dark-haired man smirked at Keziah. They all drew a deep breath, and they sang again, Tahnee's high-pitched voice joining the fray and sending them even further off the beat.

Much to Keziah's disappointment, these humans didn't have a drop of magic. There was no press of urgent or gentle influence. She didn't feel restless binding of magic across her free will.

They had nothing more than wild-eyed, bright, and eager encouragement, which worked just as well. They repeated the last word of their song, again and again and again, until Keziah realised it was her cue to drink.

She lifted the small glass to her lips, and following Tahnee's lead, she poured the whole thing down her throat. It was sharp, earthy and then it burned.

The second shot slipped from her fingers as Keziah coughed at the first, choking on the fire in her chest that warmed her from the inside out.

"Oh!" She coughed again.

The group groaned at the spilled alcohol on the floor. Keziah pressed a hand to her chest and turned away from them.

Tahnee laughed, "You wasted it!"

"Hold on tighter next time," someone said.

"I'll get her another."

Keziah wasn't waiting to drink fire again. She shook her head; the back of her hand pressed against her full lips and fled the group. Nobody protested, and by the time the next round of drinks appeared, they barely thought of her at all. Nothing unusual, really.

Keziah stood at the edge of the rooftop balcony, beneath the tiny, twinkling lights, and wondered what she was doing there. She didn't want to find a human slave. What would she even do with them, without the light of the moon, with her powers so bound by childhood lullabies? A part of her remained eager to play with them tonight and she did, indulging in the whim while the possibilities lasted. Every time a human approached; Keziah sung a soft command.

"Spin three times and touch your nose."

"Dance for me. Again. Again. Again."

"Fetch me water."

"Do it. Kiss Tahnee. Kiss her like she's the last female in your realm."

Every time they complied, her blood sizzled with a delicious warmth, adrenaline burned at the back of her throat and her skin glowed. Magic weaved through every cell of her being until, beneath the High Moon, Keziah could believe that she was nothing without it. She was more drunk on her gifts than alcohol.

Already, she mourned going back to being unworthy, being nothing at all. Three months was a long time to wait to experience it all again.

She sighed and stared down at the dark streets of Zemē. It was so bland, so unlifelike compared to the forests, mountains and tumbling, raging rivers that expanded across Solis. Where the flowers that bloomed in the day and glowed in the night. In comparison, the brick, glass, and metal of this realm felt cold and uninviting, and she had expected the people to be much the same way.

Keziah shivered, gaze wandering now that she had nobody to play with. Which was when she noticed it.

The thief. He strode down the middle of the road at the furthest end of the street, heading to pass them by. A tall male, too tall to be human, and walking at an unhurried pace. Long, white hair hung down his back, swinging with each step. The unmistakable sight of the large, curving scythe strapped to his back was the part that left Keziah inhaling sharply. It only confirmed the similarities to the thief from her parent's bedchamber.

She turned on her heel blindly, racing through the mingling humans for the strange metal box that had brought them up here. She stabbed urgently the button on the wall, like Tahnee had.

The doors slid open; the siren rushed inside, and then stared, confused, at the panel of seven or eight buttons on the wall. Which one would take her to the thief?

Tahnee had consulted the device in her pocket before she had taken them to the last button, and so hesitantly, Keziah selected all of them.

One by one, the buttons glowed as if lit by magic.

A sigh of relief slipped from her lips as the metal box shuddered and dropped. Only it stopped too soon. Sliding to a halt, the doors opening to a dark and familiar hallway. Keziah frowned, pressed against the back of the box, the metal cold against her skin.

The doors slid open; the box moved. It happened again and again. With every floor, Keziah fretted, her head spinning with the worry that he would have escaped. When the doors opened to the transparent glass panels of the building foyer and the street ahead, a frenzied sob of frustration rolled from her throat.

Keziah burst from the metal box and into the street. She glanced in the way the male had been and found it empty. Her fingers trembled by her side as she wrestled with a wave of crushing disappointment.

Then she spun, skirt flaring at her ankles, bells tinkling with the movement, and frantically, Keziah scanned the dark streets for any sign of him.

"Where are you?" She murmured. She wanted to scream the words, with the full power of her song, demand an answer from right across the city, but that was the power of a Queen and Keziah was nothing of the sort.

Stubbornly, she kicked her feet from the jewelled slippers that pinched her toes and slowed her down. Keziah stepped onto the unfamiliar, rough texture of the road.

Her hands fisted in her skirt, she lifted the hem, as not to trip, and the siren ran in the direction that the male had been moving, pausing at every intersection to peer down the dark, winding allies for a glimpse of him.

It was only once her feet ached, rubbed raw from the rough road, that she caught sight of him, the flash of moonlight white hair rounding the next corner.

Relief soothed her only for a second before Keziah realised she was losing him again. She caught her breath, sweet mouthfuls of air, and then ran again, slowing only when he was well in view.

Keziah of Quaver followed him quietly for several blocks. She watched him with curiosity, stopped when he stopped, and moved when he did.

What was the thief stealing tonight?

If the male knew she was following, he didn't give any indication of it. In fact, he never once looked over his shoulder or watched his back, only continued forward in his slow march.

He came to a halt in front of a building, and Keziah squinted up at the bright red word that flashes at the front door.

EMERGENCY.

Keziah frowned and tried to remember what the human word meant, translating it into her own language in her head as the male had walked right through the closed front door.

Keziah squeaked and hurried to follow.

When she approached, the glass slid aside automatically for her entrance. Suspicious of doors that moved on their own. She hesitated. But the male was escaping, so she found her courage and the siren crept inside.

It was quiet in the dead of night, and she hid in the shadows of the foyer, watching the humans in their strange outfits. Each one wrapped tight in blue material that fell past their knees, sat high around their necks, and hung to their wrists. Rubbery looking gloves over their fingers, caps wrapped around their hair, masks secured over their faces. They were only recognisable through their eyes, seen from behind shields of plastic.

They had tired, sad eyes.

The room had sections marked out by lines of green, orange, and red, but she couldn't work out what they meant. Keziah swallowed, unsure of what she had walked into and of what to do next.

The male walked through them as if he didn't exist. Not even one human looked at him. Some just moved out of his way, as if driven by an invisible force.

He slipped around the humans to enter rooms caged with glass, and some separated only by blue fabric curtains.

Keziah watched as a soft glow of light appeared behind the curtains, and she gasped.

Humans had magic, and he was stealing it.

When the male slipped out through one of the back doors of the room, deeper into the building, she found the courage to follow.

Barefoot and nervous, Keziah stepped into the busy room. The human looked up, catching sight of her, and their eyes widened behind the fogged plastic glasses.

"What are you doing?!" they screeched.

Panic seized the siren, a weight on her lungs, and she fought not to step back and flee.

"What?" she asked.

"This is a red zone!" The human shepherded towards Keziah, and she stumbled back a step. "Are you unwell? Do you have the virus? You're supposed to test outside!"

Instinctively, she reached for her magic. "*Stop!*"

The word came out like the lyrical crack of a whip through the air. The human froze. Keziah swallowed, watched them nervously, and they watched her with a frenzied upset that she didn't understand.

She inhaled deeply for fortified herself for what she would need to do. Keziah would have to thank the moon for the three months to come for giving her the power to do it.

"*You will not notice me.*" Her voice strengthened with the husky growl of her song, her skin shone, and her eyes raged with the storm of magic. "*None of you will notice me. You will simply let me pass.*"

When she glanced at the human again, his eyes didn't seem to focus on her face. Keziah slipped closer, right in front of his face, but even then, he didn't acknowledge her, staring right through her head as if she had born of jewelled glass instead of flesh and bone.

A sigh of sad relief slipped from her lips as Keziah realised she had made herself even more invisible than usual, the one thing she always loathed to be.

It was easier now for her to follow the same path through the busy commotion that the strange male had taken, following him into the hall.

He was waiting, standing still in a long, dark hallway, and Keziah stopped three paces from his back.

"Well, well... If it isn't the Siren Princess," the male let out an aggravated sigh. "I thought I felt your magic."

He didn't sound happy about it.

8

Death closed his eyes and willed her not to see him. The princess who stood too close and saw too much. The siren foolish enough to enter a world riddled with lifelessness just for the sake of her petty little hunt for him.

"Tell me who you are!" The siren demanded and irritation tickled down his spine at the lilt of magical command at her voice.

He spun to face her and scowling into the face of her youth and curiosity.

"That's none of your concern, Siren." Death dismissed brusquely.

Her mouth tightened with disappointment, and she bristled with obvious anger. Strangely, she jingled softly with every movement. His eyes dropped to inspect her, and he wanted to laugh at the sight of the tiny bells wrapped around her limbs. It was hard to take her anger seriously.

"Yes, it is!" The siren protested hotly, her face seeming to flush with her own audacity. "Especially if you're stealing magic!"

"I am not stealing magic, Keziah of Quaver."

Keziah stepped backwards, alarm flashed across her features before she shook her head, wild curls falling over her shoulders. She seemed to brace herself.

"How do you know who I am!?"

He snorted softly. "Again, this is not your business."

"It's my business, it's my name in your mouth," The siren moved forward and pressed boldly into his space. "My name, my business, and if you know my name, I should know yours."

Death inhaled sharply, a warning that echoed through the hall. Nobody came into his space like that without permission, and this little siren had the audacity to make demands of him.

He bared his teeth, shadows crawled up his neck, an undeniable magic.

The siren stepped back, her throat bobbled, the bells at her wrists rattled again.

He watched her closely, scoffed, and turned his back on the siren to stride back down the hall.

Death could feel the way she flinched in the shift in the air. Hear the hurt of his dismissal in the choked inhale on her lips. A smirk curled at the edges of his lips, satisfied, as he continued down the hall.

Bells rustled, tinkled and his teeth grit when she found the courage to follow him. Down the hall, and then after he passed through the next door and faced the final moments of this next soul, she ripped it open behind him.

Death turned, hissing.

The siren froze, framed in the doorway, a flash of fear stark across her features.

"Leave," Death demanded.

"No."

Death straightened, a swift and eerie movement, and stared at the siren. "I said leave."

She shook her head, her earrings rattled, and he watched the muscles in her shoulders tense as she braced herself for the fight.

Death advanced on her quickly.

Behind them, the human on the bed's breath rattled in its chest. An ominous sound that signalled he was nearing the end.

As he stalked forward, the little siren thought better of her audacity and backed up. He followed until she hit the wall.

"Better," Death growled. "But still not good enough."

The siren lifted her chin, he could see the conflict that flicked across her face and recalled the same expression in the shadows of her mother's experiences. She would wilt, just like he had seen her do in her mother's memories.

"I'm not leaving," She cleared her throat, surprising him. He felt her magic stir in the air. "You will let me stay!"

Death laughed dryly. "Your party tricks don't work on me siren."

She deflated.

He tipped up his chin and looked down his nose at the siren. She looked so young, crushed beneath this minor failure, and had he been a pitying male he might have felt something at the shattered look on her face.

"His final moments are not for you," Death told her quietly, firmly. "Find your respect and leave."

Her grey eyes flickered past him. Death shifted to block her view of the door.

"He's dying?" Her voice was sharp.

"Yes."

"What do you want with a dead man's magic?"

"I told you," Death's patience was wearing thin. "I am not stealing magic."

"What do you take from them then?" Her chin lifted, her tumultuous grey eyes holding his gaze. "What did you steal from my father?"

Death leaned low, his face an inch from hers and to her credit the siren did not flinch away. Up close, the scent of her was driving him half-crazy, he imagined if he touched her, she would be soft, compliant. Death swallowed roughly. "How badly do you want to know, Princess?"

"Tell me!"

He went preternaturally still, then nodded slowly. Death smiled, all sharp teeth, as he satiated her curiosity, "I do not steal their magic; I steal their souls."

9

Alarm pulsed through Keziah, wild and erratic in her growing desire to flee and the strange need to stay there, face to face with her invisible thief and process the secret that spilled from his lips.

"Their souls?"

He was close that she could feel the wash of his breath across her lips. His white hair spilled over his shoulders, curtaining them off from the rest of the world. The right side of his head shaved short, softly shadowed where the hair threatened to grow back. A thin braid swung from the longer side, a black feather knotted in the end.

With his hood slipped back, she could see the soft points of his ears, pierced with pieces of black opal that swirled beneath the low light. Keziah relaxed incrementally as she noted them.

"You're just fae," she stated.

Displeasure twisted across his features, thin lips lifting in a sneer as he rejected the claim without speaking.

"Ash or Argent?" Keziah asked, lifting her hand intending to brush her fingers across the soft point to of his ear.

His hand clamped suddenly around her wrist, and he slammed her against the wall.

Keziah tugged at his grip to draw it back to herself, but he held firm, pinning her there.

"Do not touch me," He hissed.

"Why not?"

The male ignored the question.

Through the still partly open door, the rattle within the human's chest fell silent.

A shudder worked through the male at the deafening new silence, and Keziah couldn't work out why.

"Ask me why I take souls..." He blurted.

A lump seemed to form in her throat. Her eyes flicked to her dirtied feet. She couldn't leave now, not as he held her in place. He offered her time and didn't talk or move as he waited for to find her courage.

Keziah prayed slightly for her sister's sunflower spine, her strength of will, her ability to stand tall.

She glanced up, nodded, jaw set stubbornly, "Why do you take their souls?"

The male smiled slowly; darkness flickered in the void of his gaze. Every hair on Keziah's body stood on end in warning. An instinctual need to flee overwhelmed her, and Keziah thrashed to pull her wrist free of his grip.

The male pressed close to her, his body moulding against her curves. Keziah felt trapped. She could feel the lean muscle of his body.

Her face pressed against the slender column of his throat; his face buried into her curls as the male held her still, trapped.

Keziah's heart skittered with fear, her body revolted with the need to move. She heard the words clearly, even though the fae male whispered them into her hair. The words her soul knew, and her mind refused to accept. The reality that forced her instinct to flee. Shadows slithered up his arms and licked against her skin.

A keening whine of fear pulled from the back of her throat.

"I am Death."

"I..." Keziah babbled, and she thrashed against him. Fighting to get free as dread slipped like ice down her spine.

"Shhh," He demanded in a silky tone. "Sleep now."

Her body weighed down like wet sand as his shadows curled against her skin. Keziah's eyes rolled in the back of her head, and she slumped against him, unconscious.

When she woke again, Keziah was in the cold halls of the human hospital. Her head pounded every time she tried to move, and she was completely alone. Death had left her in the cold hallway, unconscious.

It took a moment to find her feet, one hand pressed against the wall and the other to her head as it spun. She tried to determine if everything she could remember was real or just a fragment of her imagination. The wildest of dreams.

Slowly, Keziah edged towards the still partly open door.

The human inside lay still. Their eyes were open, vacant, dead.

A shiver rolled down her spine.

Keziah reeled backwards and started retracing her path into the busier section of the hospital. The humans still looked past her, through her, compelled to believe she wasn't there.

A bitter feeling twisted in her stomach, hot and cold all at once. Keziah twisted around the room, careful not to touch them.

"Forty-four deaths in one night," one human hissed at another. "For fuck's sake, I'm dead tired, and this virus isn't slowing."

Keziah trembled, forcing herself to breathe and admitting to herself that it his words might be true. He could reap from the deaths in this building. She had not stalked a normal fae male through the darkened streets. She had followed death on his path through Zemē. It sounded like he had had a busy night.

One glance at the street told her that the sun was rising, and a new, more urgent fear licked at the base of Keziah's spine.

If the moon were gone, disappearing beneath the soft, glowing light of the new day, she would become trapped in this realm, and Zemē was suddenly the last place she wanted to be.

Keziah burst back into the street, which was livelier now that the night was receding, and humans jogged along the paths. Her grey eyes searched the sky, painted in soft pink and a glow of orange, for the moon. The erratic staccato of her heart dulled only when she found it, faint and sinking, but still present.

She relied on instinct alone to find the park where the two realms backed onto one another, following the gentle hum of magic where like called to like.

Keziah ran as fast as she could, slippers in her hand. When she saw Thea and Quinn waiting, stress twisted into their features, human by their side.

"Kez!" Thea screeched when she noticed her, and they slammed into each other. Thea's arms wrapped around her like an iron vice, strangling the air from her chest. "Where have you been?!"

"Uhh," Keziah struggled. "I don't know, honestly."

Thea pulled back; the truth of her worry written across her face. "We thought... We thought the humans discovered you. We thought we'd lost you."

Keziah's stomach twisted; they hadn't mentioned that risk beforehand.

Quinn cleared her throat. "We need to go."

She started shepherding their humans between the trees, but they had become restless, nervous, and started mumbling about the need to get home.

"Keziah," Quinn said her name sharply. "A bit of encouragement would be nice, don't you think?"

She nodded and inhaled quickly, but when she went to speak all Keziah could think of was how her magic had failed in the face of Death. Just as her mother had always warned, she was not strong enough to be anything more than insurance for their bloodline.

The air fled from Keziah's lungs, replaced by weighted anxiety. "I can't... I'm sorry I just... can't."

Quinn scoffed. "Useless."

"Quinn!" Thea scolded. "Be nice!"

"What?" Quinn reached for the nearest humans, her fingers digging into their skin. "The one time we need some manipulation, and she can't come through? Come on!"

The Dreamous Princess used all her strength to shove them through the barrier between realms.

They screamed as they vanished. There one moment and gone the next, tossed into the light and wonder of Solis.

Quinn turned back to them, arms folded across her chest, "Disappears all night, doesn't bring a single human back with her and now she can't even help."

Without giving Keziah the chance to protest, Quinn disappeared behind her prey.

Thea sighed heavily. "She doesn't mean it, Kez."

"She does, and she's not wrong. I'm useless." Keziah whispered as Thea coaxed her new friend through the portal in the trees. "She hates me. Everyone hates me."

Thea's smile dropped. "She's just worried. I was worried, too, Kez. You just disappeared, we thought we'd lost you."

Keziah sighed, nodding glumly. Thea entwined their fingers, the weight of her hand familiar and reassuring. "Let's go home."

They stepped back into Solis, together.

10

Frustration had taken up permanent residence within his body, leaving him agitated. It reflected in the ominous storms that rolled through Iriya, lightening crackling through the skies.

Death grit his teeth and paced back and forth through the long halls of his residence. Forged from the gleaming black opal found in the earth of his realm and when the flickering of candlelight hit the polished stones and they threw off flashes of red, blue, and gold.

The doors to his dining room flew open as he pushed his way inside, where Death found Yael seated in his spot at the head of the table.

The angel of light was more corporeal than usual, sporting an androgynous appearance, with her legs kicked up and settled next to a gold plate.

"How," Yael barely looked up as they spoke. "Do you anticipate that the souls in my care get everlasting rest and peace for eternity when you're setting off storms across the entire plane?"

Death growled. He stalked forward and swept his arm at Yael's legs, shoving them away. "Get your feet off my fucking table."

A loud crunch echoed from beside him, and Death spun to find Jael with his teeth caught in the side of a bright red apple.

"You were right," Jael said to Yael over Death's shoulder. "He is in a horrible mood."

"I'm always right."

"You are not!"

"Of course, I am. Just look at him. He's—"

"Out!" With a snarl, Death pointed to the door.

Neither of them moved, and discomfort breathed down his neck as they scrutinised him.

"Leave!" He spat. "Now!"

"The last face of Death," Yael sniffed. "Was much nicer than you, you know."

Death rolled his eyes. "The last death was a human woman who barely lasted thirty years with the shadows before they sent her wild."

Jael nodded in agreement and bit into the apple again. "He's not wrong."

"Yet for all her quick existence, she was still a much nicer person to deal with!" Yael protested shrilly. "You need to stop taking your petty tantrums out on Iriya."

Death sighed, turning his back on them. When he glanced over his shoulder, Yael still sat in his chair, elbows perched on the table, her full focus on him.

He wrenched out another from beneath the table and dropped heavily into it, and grumbled, "I'm not doing it intentionally."

"We know," Yael and Jael said in unison. "But..."

Death massaged his temples and the ache that brewed there. They both studied him. He groaned. "Go on then..."

"Something must be on your mind, Grim?" Jael dropped into another of the seats and set the half-chewed apple onto one of the golden plates. It rocked and settled.

"What is it?" Yael asked.

Death closed his eyes and counted to three.

When he opened them, the angels hadn't disappeared, much to his disappointment. He ground his teeth together, settled back and stared at the table like a sullen youth, willing food into existence.

A platter of fruit appeared between them all

That was Iriya, a plane that connected to the mind of the current face of Death, bearer of shadows. There were four territories of Iriya: The Triplean Fields, The Oplean Underground, Varelle City, and the Solitary Walk. The entire realm shaped and perfected by the force of his will, food appeared when he wanted, the palace-like residence he maintained shifting to whatever he may need, and when his thoughts raged, so did the skies and the rivers.

After two weeks of restless weather and the cities reshaping themselves, the souls who lived here with him had had enough. There was no other reason that Yael and Jael would have arrived in Varelle City. Each one visited from time to time, but hardly ever entered his opal palace uninvited, respecting the need for his own space.

"Or who is it?" Jael asked, a little more astute than his lighter counterpart.

Death narrowed his eyes at him, and Jael grinned widely.

"Danye?" He guessed.

"No."

"Grim, you don't have any other friends..."

"The demon queen is not my friend," Death hissed between clenched teeth, cold fury intermingling with the annoyance on his slender features.

"Ah," Yael chimed in. "Our mistake."

He picked up an orange, sliding his thumb beneath the rough skin and peeling the juicy segments of fruit free if it.

Light and darkness both waited for him. Everyone in this realm waited on him, and none of them, he thought, truly saw him either. He was a necessity, but not truly wanted.

Death sighed heavily. "There's a female."

Yael gasped. "Who?"

He ignored that question. "When I am in other realms, she sees me."

"So?"

He pinned the embodiment of lightness beneath a glare, and her glow dimmed.

"I only meant that we see you. Souls see you. Danye sees you." Yael corrected. "You're not invisible to everyone."

"I am when I'm reaping."

Silence lingered between them before Jael disagreed. "Not always."

Death stilled, juice from the orange dripping down his wrist.

"There was that human one time. She's in with me? What did they call her? A medium? She believed she could see the spirits; she could see you."

Sharp teeth ripped into the flesh of the orange. Juice dripped down the point of his chin. Death swallowed before he answered. "But she couldn't actually see me."

"Right..." Jael agreed. "Maybe this woman is pretending, too."

Death discarded the orange. Suddenly, it tasted like ash against his tongue. "No."

"Are you sure?"

"Of course, I'm sure. I'm not a child picking out what he wants for breakfast."

"It's just..." Jael protested.

"I spoke to her," Death stated firmly. "I touched her; she could see me."

Yael dropped the fork they had been twirling between her fingers. It clattered against the golden plate. "You touched her?"

"That's what I said, isn't it?"

"Touched her how?"

Death was silent. He let their imaginations run wild. It was better that way, and a moment later Yael let out a muffled giggle, sign enough that both of their imaginations lay in the gutter.

"It's not the first time she's seen me," he admitted, ignoring the laughter.

'Who is it?" Jael asked.

"Keziah," He muttered her name beneath his breath. A curse of its own. They both looked blankly at Death. Not a flicker of recognition between them.

"The Second Princess of the Solisan Quaver Court."

"So?" Yael frowned. "What's wrong with a daughter of Solis being able to see you?"

"I—" He had no explanation.

"It doesn't affect you," Yael continued.

"Yes, but—"

"She's not fae, either, which, if she was, I could understand how that would rankle you. But a Siren..."

"It's more—"

"You could just ignore her," Yael cut over him. "Since she makes absolutely no difference to your life, or your work, and is completely unworthy of the harsh weather you've forced us to endure. They souls say it feels like it's gone on a century."

Death slammed both fists down on the table, hard. Gold plates rattled, a crystal goblet teetered before it fell, spilling a dark wine across the table.

Yael jumped, and he bared his teeth in warning.

"I just want to know why!"

"Hmm," Jael picked up his apple. They tossed it in the air, caught it swiftly and took another crunching bite. "Didn't you take her parents recently?"

Death stilled in his rage; his eyes cut to the darker of the two, waiting for him to continue.

Jael took his sweet time. "Why not just ask them?"

J ael's domain in Iriya was a chilly place, the Oplean Underground. It comprised a series of caverns and caves built into the core of the realm, prisons shaped from the pretty gems of which souls could not cross, the black opal. It was the perfect containment while they repented.

It was the worst of the four realms of prisons, punishment served, and penance received to shape souls into better outcomes in their next lives.

Each punishment was unique to the soul, served in a cell kept only for them. The souls here did not live freely as they did with Yael. They did not cross mingle, but remained in isolation. Penance was a lonely confinement.

Jael whistled a jaunty tune as he led his way to the cell. In the distance, a cacophony of screams played out in Death's ears, screams and pleas from the souls within.

"This one," Jael announced. "Kalliah of Quaver, Solis. One thousand Solis years."

Death walked through the gemstone walls and into the cold metal cube. The illusions of Kalliah's penance dimmed, everything dimmed away until it was just them, and the soft glow of light that was an old queen's soul bobbed and shifted until it took the form of the life had just experienced. This form would be hard for her soul to forget after thousands of years of existing within it.

Death could see the similarities between mother and daughter.

"Come set me free, Shadow Lord!" Kalliah cried, unable to stop herself from issuing it as a command. The words sounded scratchy and painful, all the wrong notes, and it caused Death to grit his teeth. The dead queen flinched back from her own words.

"No." Death didn't hesitate to reject the command. "I'm here to talk to you about your daughter."

"Kalani," the soul hissed and shot forward towards death, screaming her commands and they sounded like nails scraped against rock. "You will not take her early! I forbid it! Do you hear me?!"

Death reached for the soul, the shadows on his fingers wrapping around it tightly. The soul lost its chosen shape, shifting and shrinking until it fit neatly into the palm of his hand.

He squeezed hard, shadows slipping from his skin, wrapping around his hands, caging the soul in and Kalliah screamed in genuine pain every time they touched.

"You make no demands of me."

"No," she whimpered in remorse. "No, not at all."

He let go. The soul bobbed to the far corner of the glittering room, and only then did it reform its shape.

Death glared at Kalliah.

"You daughter—"

"My penance," Kalliah hissed. "Is that I cannot use my voice for a thousand years?"

"And?"

"Yet here I am, speaking to you, which should be impossible." She hissed, but he offered no explanation. "Which daughter?"

"Keziah."

The queen's face formed long enough for Death to see the cruel smile that twisted across her face, the way her form glowed with emotion. "What about her?"

"Tell me about her."

"You've met Keziah?" The soul hissed. "I'm glad she's dead."

"She's not," Death spat.

He could feel the disappointment from the soul and demanded, "Tell me everything about Keziah."

The soul smirked, a vile expression on the scraps left of a vile woman. When she laughed, it scraped along his nerves, the rise and fall of her voice agitating him.

"No," Kalliah refused. "I think I'll serve my penance instead."

The soul said not another word.

When Death stormed out, he snarled at Jael to triple her sentence.

On the walk back to Varelle City, Death paused at the crossroads and stared out at the emptiness of the pathways that led to rest, penance, or rebirth. Halfway down the path to rebirth, he could see the soft glow of a soul lingering by the edge of the path.

Death waited. It didn't move.

A growl rolled from the back of his throat, primal and fae, and Death strode brusquely down the path to stand by the lost soul. It didn't shy away from him.

"Who are you?" Death demanded.

The soul shifted and found a shape. Death frowned at the face, trying to place the name among the thousands of souls he had released along this path. It took him a moment.

"Nivean of Solis," the soul aided him.

"Ah," Death nodded. "Why are you still here? You stepped down this path quite some time ago."

Or so he thought. It was hard to keep track in Iriya, but there had been many souls since this one, many who must have passed him on this path and overtaken him in the journey to another chance. Footsteps he did not follow.

"I'm nervous," the soul confessed. "Worried that my new life will be just as tormented as my old one."

"As a King Consort?" Death remarked, not unkindly. "Many would consider that a position of great fortune."

The soul dimmed in the reflection of its own trauma, and Death sighed heavily. They stood in silence, before Death tucked his fingers into his pockets and dipped his chin.

"Nivean, I cannot make promises that your next life will be better, but it will be much freer without Kalliah in it."

The soul of Nivean shivered at the sound of his queen's name, at the insult implied in the statement.

That was the problem with the Quaver Sirens, with enough power their commands did not just influence the unconscious thought path, or the brain, instead they settled like iron chains across the soul. Nivean may always be bound by Kalliah.

"What am I to do with freedom, then?"

"Whatever you want," Death said simply. "The world is yours for the taking. That, Nivean, is the beauty of the path of the Solitary Walk and the rebirth that comes at the end. You get to begin again."

The soul processed his words and bobbed in soft agreement. Nivean said no more, but drifted further down the Solitary Walk, headed for his new life.

"Wait!" Death called, just before Nivean slipped from sight. The soul hesitated. "I have a question."

"What about?"

"Your daughter," Death admitted.

"Kalani or Keziah."

"Keziah," Death breathed her name like a curse. "Your daughter can see me when I am all but invisible to most. She sees through the shadows that keep me hidden and she calls me out. Why is that?"

The soul turned and drew closer again. Death could see the expression of regret on the softly lit form it had taken.

"Kalliah has told that girl since birth that she is destined only for death, and she has never truly lived." Nivean confessed. "She slipped it into her lullabies as a maid rocked her to sleep. She sung it daringly to her face. Since Keziah was born, she has been in wait for her sister's ascension and her own death."

Death mulled the statement over; the impact of a Quaver Queen's song had remained as scars on souls since long before he was the face and commander of Iriya.

The soul backed away, edging towards his new destiny but as he disappeared, he called back to the rigid male on the path.

"My Keziah can see you," He advised. "Because she has waited her whole life for death."

11

Three days after the High Moon and there were humans wandering throughout Solis, captured by Sirens, Fae, and Mer alike, all of whom indulged.

The sirens courts remained together at Quaver Castle; the coronation ceremony of Queen Kalani of Quaver was, once again, delayed as each of the courts indulged their fill with the new human's sacrifices. When they were all filled with magic, the time would come for revelry.

Keziah could barely walk down the halls of the castle without finding Carnality Sirens in dark corners fucking humans until they glowed with both orgasm and power.

At night, the Dreamous Sirens ran rampant. More than once, Keziah found herself lost in an errant dream and bore witness to the nightmares of man. Humans had horrifying imaginations, but the Dreamous sirens seemed to thrive off it.

As for her own court, the Quaver sirens were not as blatant when they fed, but there was a glow of healthiness and power among all, especially the queen.

Queen Kalani now always kept a pair of humans with her, collared and secured to jingling leashes like hounds, and often to the amusement of the court. She had them perform little party tricks, dancing for their amusement. She basked in the way their compliance stoked her power, and, in the attention, she received for it. She had never seemed so strong.

Keziah's power, in comparison, waned without the strength of the moon behind to boost it. While humans were undeniably easier to influence than those who wielded magic, she struggled to get them to follow even the most basic of commands. It chipped away at her confidence. It left her quiet, withdrawn, and thinking of the other male she could not influence.

She had always thought that death was an occurrence and not a being; and now that she knew it was both, it made sense. Where else would the essence of someone go if not collected?

The male had not stolen her mother's magic, Kalani's ever-growing power proved that it had ascended to the next heir, no he had collected their souls and Keziah now burned with desperate curiosity about what he did with them once he had them. Where did the souls go next?

He stayed on her mind throughout the long days and even longer nights. Quinn and Thea had forgiven her for disappearing, more so when she revealed she had followed the fae male down the streets of Zemē. They teased her about it, Quinn bringing a distorted version of him to life in her dreams for giggles.

It was never quite right, though; he was softer in those make-believe dreams. The harsh edge to him disappearing beneath the fact that the dream version of Death wanted her there, instead of watching on with ill-concealed disgust that she was there at all. Softened by romantic notions from Quinn and Thea and losing the tiny details she had never told them.

He haunted her thoughts, and the worst bit was that Keziah knew that death would not think of her at all. History did not keep the names of second princesses in their records, and sirens did not stop to think on them at all. Keziah was sure that death was no exception to this rule.

At dinner she sat at the end of the royal table, beside Thea, watching as young siren males waltzed to the front of the table and clamoured for Queen Kalani's attention, each wishing to prove they could provide her with the next healthy heir.

"I like that one," Thea commented, tilting her head at the dark-haired Carnality male that tried his luck. He leaned in close and whispered in Queen Kalani's ear, something that made her blush. "In fact, I think I've had him."

This drew Keziah's attention, and she studied the male, unable to stop herself from comparing his dark, pale features to those of the fae male, Death.

"Kalani will reject him..." she murmured.

Thea scoffed disbelieving but sure enough, a moment later, Queen Kalani flicked her fingers and the male's shoulders sagged before he sloped away.

"Tell me why!?" Thea demanded.

"He's not Quaver..."

Thea looked insulted. "So?"

"The late queen always told Kalani she must choose only Quaver; so, the next Princess might have a more powerful song. Kalani knows her duty."

Thea's nose scrunched up. "How stupid."

"Like your mother wouldn't do anything for power?" Keziah shot back, and they both looked at Queen Elvira. She sat beside Kalani, the vision of sensuality, her lips painted in a striking, attractive shade of red.

It was no wonder half the approaching males flicked their gaze her way despite themselves. She may have been older, and not the Queen available to them, but she was still alluring.

"Except take a king," Thea said and stabbed her fork into a piece of meat. "That's the one thing she'll never do."

They lapsed into silence, watching the rigmarole three times over before Keziah had had enough. She pushed back her chair. It scraped loudly against the stone floor, attracting attention. Eyes lingered on her, including that of all three siren Queens. She blushed deeply.

Keziah cleared her throat and bowed her head in deference to them. "If you'll excuse me."

"Yes, indeed. I excuse you, Princess Keziah." Kalani agreed in a bored tone that lit a hot flush of embarrassment across Keziah's cheeks.

Soft giggles swept through the room. Keziah's throat bobbed, and she straightened slowly. It took all her strength of will to not to glance back as she strode down the hall.

"**K**eziah!" At the sound of her sister's voice, the second princess faltered and turned. It wasn't something she could simply ignore. Her skirts spun at her ankles, and she smoothed her palms against them, sweeping across the patterns of deep green and gold to settle the material.

She stood, waiting, as Queen Kalani took her time to approach, stepping down the hall with slow purpose. All the while making Keziah wait.

It was a familiar pastime, waiting in the shadows for the moment someone would look her way, waiting for the breath in the middle of the conversation where she might interject with her own thoughts. Waiting for acknowledgement.

The queen came to a stop in front of her, reaching out to straighten the fragile gold diadem pressed to Keziah's forehead.

"Next time," Queen Kalani clicked her tongue, and she seemed far over two years older than Keziah. "*You will remain in your seat until I have given you leave. You will not draw attention to yourself.*"

Keziah's lungs squeezed tight. It sounded like Kalani was simply talking, barely a lilt of power to her voice. Despite that, she could feel the uncomfortable web of magic grating against her soul. The manipulation in the command.

She let out a breathless squeak of protest. "You don't need to do that!"

"Do what?" Queen Kalani asked cheekily.

"Force me to obey, Kala." She whispered. "I'd do what you asked. I'd do it for you. I always have."

Queen Kalani shook her head. "Mother always said—"

"Queen Kalliah was wrong!" Keziah hissed. "And a terrible mother."

Those words lingered in the space between the two sisters raised and treated completely differently by their family, one favoured while the other forgotten.

Keziah watched as turmoil flicked in her sister's stormy gaze and then hardened into granite resolve. She had always been strong, Queen Kalani of Quaver with the sunflower spine.

The Queen rose to her full height; she lifted her chin and the jewels that hung from the lobes of her ears tinkled as they swung with the movement. "You need to learn your place, Keziah."

Hot tears pooled in her eyes and rolled down Keziah's cheek. She brushed a curl from her face with the back of her hand.

"I know my place."

"Do you?" Queen Kalani sneered.

An emotional wall crumbled inside Keziah and despite the way tears rolled down her face at the confrontation, she fisted her hands in her skirts. She lifted her chin.

"Yes," she all but sobbed the word. Keziah drew a breath and mimicked her mother's sharp tones, the words coming out in a rush. "Second princess. Utterly unnecessary. Unworthy of power, unworthy of a voice. Always in the way. Seen and not heard. Not to get in Kalani's way, not to touch Kalani, not to speak ill of Kalani. Not to draw attention, seen and not heard.

To wait for my sister to become queen, to wait for her to find a consort, to wait for her to birth to next queen... To wait for my death. My place is—"

Queen Kalani's hand struck her cheek so hard that Keziah tasted the bitterness of blood, and her head rang.

"Stop it," her sister hissed.

Keziah glared at her through wet lashes. "Don't you like the truth, sister?"

"Stop it," the queen repeated. "You are not hard done by Keziah, you are a princess of Quaver."

Keziah's throat bobbed. "And?"

"Be grateful!"

"*Of what*?" Keziah shouted. "Of my being controlled?! Having no power?! Why am I to be grateful?"

"You may have no voice, but people see you, Keziah. You are the princess with the sweet lips and the heart-shaped face, with the spring of life in everything she does. You are free to be joyful, albeit not to be queen."

If she hadn't known any better, Keziah might have thought that Queen Kalani was jealous of her, but she shook her head. Her palms rubbed over her face, smearing the dots of gold kohl applied for dinner, fingers tangling in her curls. When she looked up again, her face was haunted.

"Am I to understand that I live a life of restriction, but I should grateful that people look at me on occasion and that mother allowed me to laugh? Because you think that one of your precious suitors glanced my way instead of yours?"

Queen Kalani pressed her lips together, a raging storm rolled behind her eyes.

"Fine, have it your way."

Keziah didn't like it, the sharp way the word rolled off the end of her tongue. She stepped back, bells at her ankles jingling softly.

"Kalani," Keziah warned.

"That's Queen Kalani to you."

Keziah flinched.

Her sister reached for her, firmly gripping her wrist. Instinctively, she flinched back, old magic pushing her to release the contact and it left her antsy, her skin itching. Since ten years old, Keziah hadn't touched Kalani, when her older sister had convinced her to take scissors. Their mother hadn't liked that one bit, when her heir had turned up to dinner with ravaged curls.

The queen dragged her closer, Keziah going limp as she stumbled forward, her eyes still lingered on the place where they touched, panic welling in her chest at the contact. Their skin an identical shade of umber, but as always, their similarities were only skin deep.

Keziah flinched as Queen Kalani gripped her chin, her skin pinched against one of the layered rings her sister wore.

"Sweet, Keziah," Queen Kalani hummed.

Keziah grit her teeth, hearing the power in her tone, cringing away from it.

"If you cannot be appreciative of what you do have..." Keziah closed her eyes, blocked it out. She felt Kalani brush her fingertips down her face, drawing her gaze open, forcing her to meet her fate.

"Don't, Kala, *please don't.*" Keziah didn't know what was coming, but it was easy to beg for mercy when she had been practicing it her entire life.

Queen Kalani smiled, full of teeth, and shadowed with vindictiveness. When she spoke again the echo of her power rattled the brightly painted windows as it swept across the castle.

"*No siren within this castle and these grounds will see nor acknowledge you for thirty days.*" At the Queen's decree Keziah let out a wail, an echo of pain.

"Don't..." She whispered, begged.

Her sister smirked. "See that you learn some appreciation in that time, Princess Keziah."

12

Summons came from the depths of the Demon Realm and shook Death from a period of restless slumber. He never truly slept, not when the cries of souls called to him all through the night, but sometimes he liked to lie in his large bed and pretend that sleep would come for him.

Hot, blue flames burst to light in his polished and un-used fireplace, and Danye's hissing voice interrupted the quiet of the night. "Morphosis comes early, Death. We need you."

He rolled from the large bed, landing lightly on his feet, and hunted down a shirt.

As he buttoned it, Death cleared his throat, "Jael."

Darkness flickered and appeared in his bedchambers instantaneously, Jael moved between forms, not solid, with one foot in Varelle City and one still lingering in the Oplean Underground.

Death growled. "Your attention would be appreciated."

Jael solidified, frowning as they stepped fully into the space. "I can't always just leave at your beck and command, Grim. I was dealing with someone."

"Don't call me that."

"Grim." Jael taunted.

Death growled again and turned his back on Jael, making him wait. He found a jacket on the floor and pulled it on quickly, before stalking towards one of the closets and reaching inside for his scythe. Wrought of an opal handle, the sharp curve of the blade glinted under the light. Sharp and deadly.

"You're going out?" Jael frowned; surprise coloured the roughness of his voice. "You just came back, Grim. You can't work yourself into a grave."

"Technically," Death rotated the scythe in his grip, the flames in the fireplace reflecting off it. "That is impossible."

"Ha-ha," Jael mocked dryly. "You know what I mean."

Death narrowed his eyes on Jael, who snapped his jaw shut at the look in his eye. "Danye called."

Jael blinked before he erupted into a howl of laughter that bounced off the polished walls of the room.

"What?" Death snapped from behind grit teeth.

"You're taking the Scythe on a hook-up," Jael chuckled darkly. "How delightfully kinky, Grim"

Death looked from the cackling representation of penance to the blade in his palm and considered running him through with it. It would be satisfying to see him split in two and to know it would take him more than a decade to reform, but sadly he didn't have time for such fun.

"No."

"You really are," Jael howled. "Wait until I tell Yael!"

The growl that rolled from Death this time was pure warning, low and husky, filled with layers of vengeance. The laughter in Jael's throat dissipated in an instant, his face turning serious and grave.

"Morphosis is here."

Jael's lips parted. His form flickered from the androgynous figure they preferred into something slimmer, sinister, darker, closer to the true form of the angel. "This early? It's decades before it's time."

Death nodded solemnly. "Too early."

"That's not a good sign, Grim."

He grunted since that was obvious.

"You have the power to rearrange your underground until the time I return," He commanded, and the realm shook beneath their feet at the transference of power. Rocking the opal earth as it fought the change and settling once it accepted.

"Be prepared," Death warned, he tightened his grip around the scythe and when he moved for the door, his footsteps were loud in the quiet of the realm. "I'll be back."

"Grim?"

He paused and turned back to Jael. He waited.

"Beware your demon brothers. Be safe."

Shadows lit and wreathed Death's hands, they rolled up his arms, threatening to devour him. The shadowy figure standing in his place laughed, a soft, cruel sound.

"I need no reminder, Jael." Death snapped. "And I have no brothers, no family."

A look of devastation crossed the dark angel's face but he wiped it away quickly. Without bidding him goodbye, or giving himself time to interpret that look, Death stepped fluidly from one realm to the next.

13

Keziah paced back and forth between the walls of her quarters and wanted to scream with frustration. Once, she did, screaming aloud as if she were under attack. The doors burst open, a serving girl raced inside, face twisted with fear and eyes wild. She searched for the source of the noise, but her eyes skimmed right over Keziah. They flickered past her as if she didn't see her at all, even as the princess stood right at the end of her nose.

When she couldn't find a disturbance, she left, and Keziah was alone again. A loneliness that felt like the weight of Solis on her shoulders and threatened to suffocate.

The first time it happened, she had thought it was a trick, told herself that it was easy for one person not to see her, until she turned up at the mid-week Ladies Luncheon in the courtyard, among a mixture of Siren nobility and their human slaves, and not a single person seemed to settle their eyes on her, not a single person acknowledged her presence.

When she spoke, Thea had lifted her head, turning to look for the source of her voice, but still she hadn't been able to see her, and had nudged Quinn, asking if the other Princess knew where she had gone. Nobody rose to search for her, though, turning back to their drinks.

It was then that Keziah's heart had cracked a little, and she realised the enormity of Queen Kalani's power. True to her word, she had made her completely invisible. A punishment like no other.

Now three days into her newfound invisibility, she drifted through the halls like a ghost, and had confined herself to her rooms. Unable to bear the way her heart squeezed, and the tears flowed whenever someone lifted their head and looked right through where she stood.

She paced back and forth, trying to work out a solution to her problems, but thirty days felt like a lifetime. Thirty days of being unseen and Keziah was sure she would whittle away to nothing at all.

The servants delivered food to her rooms like clockwork, Queen Kalani's way of keeping her alive, and when the servants came to take the trays away, they all remarked that the second princess must be dancing through the halls somewhere because she always ate her fill.

On the third day, she hovered around her maid and a serving girl as they remade her bed.

"It's just unusual," her maid, Juliette, murmured. "I've not seen her in days. This has never happened before; Princess Keziah doesn't just run off."

The serving girl giggled brightly. "She's likely off with someone from Carnality court, enjoying herself. I would be if we didn't have to work."

Juliette pressed her lips together, unhappy with the comment, her eyes cutting across the room as if to find a clue. "Perhaps."

"Caught in a lover," the girl sighed as they tucked the sheets in tightly. "I bet she's finally found someone who makes her heart race."

"It would be good for that girl to lose herself in someone, for once." Juliette agreed reluctantly.

The thought gave Keziah pause. She dropped softly into one of the plush loveseats to the left of the room and ignored them. They murmured in the background, fluffing pillows and reorganising as Keziah tried to determine if they were right.

Had anyone ever made her heart truly race?

She wasn't an innocent. You couldn't be friends with the second Princess of Carnality Court and remain untouched, but Keziah had never found the interest to stay longer than one dalliance and had never sought someone out again, and again, and again. Their touches had been nice, but they never left her breathless, with her heart racing and the excited desire to see them as soon as possible.

The only person she could think of that had set her heart aflutter had been Death, and she sure that was only because of his likelihood to end her own life. Or because he was a forbidden entity, shrouded in shadow.

She flopped back onto the loveseat, stared at the roof, and thought of the way he had looked at her, seen her in a way that others hadn't. The way her heart had hammered a thousand times harder with his body pressed against her own, his warm breath flushing against her skin.

If anyone could see her now, it would be him, because he truly looked. Or so she thought.

Keziah lamented him not walking through the halls of her home like any other male she could have wanted. She couldn't turn around a corner and find Death lingering by the library or staring out the window.

There would be no death to invite him into the realm. Not with the influx of humans in Solis, when the sirens had fed and were healthier than ever. It would be an eon before Death had an excuse to visit Quaver court next.

Keziah wandered aimlessly through the halls of the castle. While had felt stifled in years past, under Queen Kalliah's reign, when she had watched from afar but not taken part in anything, but it was nothing akin to the reality of being invisible.

Beneath the tight bonds of Queen Kalani's curse, Keziah had nothing to do. She followed her friends on their escapades, until she realised they wouldn't seek her out, and incite a vengeful mission to find out where she had gone. They had eyes for only one another, too engrossed in their feelings to offer her more than a brief, passing thought.

When she followed her sister, lingering in the background and rolling her eyes as the new Queen gasped and cooed over the pretty favours she received in an attempt at courting, Keziah thought she might just die of boredom.

There had to be better things to do, but she stood too quickly and knocked into a glass vase. It rocked one way and another, teetering on the edge of the table before it fell to the ground.

It shattered, but when everyone looked, there was nobody nearby. Their eyes glazed over when they looked at her, not seeing the culprit. Keziah would have laughed, if not for the narrow-eyed suspicion on the Queen's face.

Before Kalani could draw breath enough to curse her again. She fled.

Another few days passed as Keziah explored her home without notice. Long days as she whispered to herself, noting the secrets she knew about Quaver Castle. Her fingers trembled every time someone's gaze seemed to linger and flick onwards. Until she shook, and stood nose to nose with people, wishing that they would open their eyes and see what was right in front of them.

A male bumped into her when he turned, and she didn't move out of the way quickly enough. Keziah gasped. He stumbled and fell to the floor.

His friends burst into rambunctious laughter. The male's eyes flicked right over her once, but his eyes didn't focus, and Keziah began to weep as he picked himself up off the floor and brushed off his shirt.

"Tripped over your ego, Farren," he laughed flippantly.

His friend turned red. "Or your big, clumsy feet."

Within time, all Keziah could think of was Death. The male and not the fate that had long awaited her. Her pulse fluttered with a desperate longing for acknowledgement. Even if it was by a male who sneered every time he saw her, a flash of surprise and disgust in his gaze each time she had approached him.

Keziah walked the length of the hallway outside her rooms like a broken-hearted widow, alone and forgotten. As she paced, she moved out of the way of the young serving girl that helped tidy her room, make her bed, and deliver food.

The girl laughed and chattered as she worked, saying nothing of importance beyond simple court gossip, but animated with a sense of life that filled Keziah with a head spinning jealousy. She wished she could feel as this girl did, overworked but more importantly, seen.

Occasionally, the girl could pause, catching the whisper of Keziah talking to herself, and glance around, but at the sight of the empty halls, she could continue with her day.

"Where are you, Death?" She groaned by mid-afternoon, frustration leaving the muscles in her back tight, a growing headache at her temples. "Come and play with me..."

The serving girl had paused at the top of the stairs with a silver tea tray balanced heavily in her arms. It contained the leftovers of Keziah's lunch, half-eaten sandwiches, and spilled sugar from a sloppily made cup of tea.

"Who's there?" The girl whispered. Her face had paled, like she genuinely believed in ghosts.

"Me," Keziah called back and watched as an ominous shivered rolled down the girl's spine. She crept towards the girl, moving close enough that her breath should have washed over the servants' cheeks. "It's me."

"I don't have time for ghosts," he girl warned. "I don't owe anything to the spirit world."

"Not even for me?" Keziah whispered, at her back now, and the girl shivered again when Keziah's breath brushed over the back of her neck. The princess could see the panic that started to flicker in her clear blue eyes, her muscles bunching.

"It's bad omens to speak to the dead!" The girl proclaimed loudly, and Keziah realised she was reminding herself, not speaking to ghost she believed to be present.

"Yes, you're right," Keziah whispered. "Talking to the dead invites death itself."

She acted before she could overthink the plan forming in her mind. Keziah pressed her palms firmly between the girl's shoulder blades and shoved forward as hard as she could.

The tray clattered as it fell from the girl's hands and teapot shattered. Shards of porcelain flying in every direction.

Keziah stepped forward, dread and remorse swelling in her heart, and a piece of the teapot sliced her bare foot, drawing blood.

The girl toppled forward before Keziah could catch her, unbalanced and unable to right herself. She landed awkwardly on the stairs, a loud crunch echoing into the hall as her neck twisted the wrong way on impact, before the weight of her body sent her rolling down, down, down.

The serving girl lay crumpled, unmoving, and completely lifeless at a carpeted landing halfway between Keziah's wing and the next level.

A bitten apple had rolled to a stop beside her body, both sat still and damaged in the quiet hallway.

Keziah glanced down at her own hands and stared at them in wonder. Her heart raced, and a strange wonder heated her body. She had done that; she had taken the life from another person's body.

When she lifted her head up to peer at the body again, her grey eyes were alight with a forbidden sense of delight, a soft smile pulled at the corner of her lips.

Now Death would have to come.

14

Danye, Queen of Demons, had been in her position for as long as the last three faces of Death. She had long since reigned in the realm of shadows, and souls whispered tales of her shining scales and unforgiving eyes. Beneath her reign, demons were born and released among the four realms, wreaking a chaos that fuelled Kihnes. Death did not think himself special to stand by her side in the middle of the Sholheim Rift, the adjoining point between all four realms, as they watched the Morphosis begin.

Demons weren't born in the same way as Humans, Fae, Mer, or Sirens. They were a race unique to themselves. No two demons were the same. Demons emerged from the energy pulled of all four realms, the peace, and horrors across all races. Once a millennium the Sholheim Rift developed, a shift in magic that allowed them to develop their true form and from it and the demons were born, tumbling into Kihnes.

The Demoness Queen was the one who decided which she could accept into her precise balance of power. Those she did not want, she killed.

Death was on standby to collect their souls.

"You were born of the rift," Danye commented, as they stood side by side, mutually exhausted, and stared into the inky blackness above. "On one of our blackest nights."

"So, you've told me," Death did not believe the story.

"I accepted you, Fae of Shadows. I sent you to grow among your own kind when I could have killed you."

"Ah," Death rolled his eyes and forced himself not to bite back the remark that the Fae were not his own kind, else they would never have rejected him so easily. "But then you'd never have enjoyed every inch of me."

Danye chuckled, a sensual serpentine sound. Her red eyes flicked in his direction, but movement in the rift stopped her next remark.

A shadow-hound prowled from the darkness, sharp teeth bared and a growl echoing from the back of its throat.

Danye crouched low, dipping into an offensive stance. Her chin tipped up, eyes glowing with challenge as the snakes on her crown hissed and coiled, ready to strike. Her forked tongue flicked, tasting the air.

The gorgon and the hellhound stared at each other for a moment, communicating in ways that Death would never understand. The canine huffed and dropped low, conceding to the gorgon. Danye let out a scoff.

"Go, run," She flicked her hand, sharp nails showing where to go and the hellhound let out an almighty howl, entering her realm. The sound of it lingered in the night.

The next demon to form shifted from body to body, heavy and slow in their movements, not pausing in one shape long enough to for proper identification. The demon looked them up and down, the Gorgon and Death, before it shifted into a replica of Danye.

She didn't give it the honour of a challenge before she attacked, flying into the shadows. Death could hear the way her nails raked against flesh. Black demon blood splattered against his skin, flecked across his face, and when she returned Danye's scales were slick with it.

Death strode forward, unsheathing the scythe from his back. The blade carved through the shadows as he swept it in a wide arc through the demon muck left behind, and when he righted his weapon, a soul pierced on the tip.

He pulled an opal orb from his pocket and reached for the soul, unhooking it with ease, his jaw tightening as he lived through the feeling of Danye's fangs shredding the life from the demon.

"I hate shapeshifters," Danye commented. She had, by far, let in more new demons this century than ever before, and released more evil beings into the other worlds than he thought entirely necessary. It wasn't his place to comment on it, though.

"Why?" Death asked, peering over his shoulder at the demoness, and she shrugged.

He watched as she wiped blood from her scales and scoffed, giving her time. As like anyone else across the four realms, Danye did, in fact, like to talk.

"Last one I let through imitated me and tried to turn my entire realm against me. I won't stand for it."

Death remained silent; he did not agree nor disagree either way. Instead, he turned his face back to the rift.

It had been five demon-days now since Danye had called him here and still; they stumbled through, born from the darkness, seeking a place across the realms.

A face appeared in the shadows. Death stilled and looked them in the eyes.

"Human," Danye called. "Let them pass."

The man strode past Death, head high, a sneer worked onto his lips, and Danye circled him in slow inspection. Her face lifted, golden eyes flicking to Death. "Send him to his realm."

Death pursed his lips. His gaze flicked over the man and a growl rolled from the back of his throat. He could feel the taint of the shadows on his soul. The way they called to his own brothers in shadow, this man was evil. He would be a taint on the humans, and he knew his actions would bring Death calling.

He hesitated to act.

"My realm, my judgement," Danye reminded him with a hiss. All her snakes bared their fangs in unsubtle warning. "You can judge him when he reaches Iriya."

Death could feel the ache in his jaw from the way teeth ground together. He did not argue, because politics between the four realms was a dangerous game to enter and he stayed out of it.

"Fine," He grunted.

Death stepped forward. His hand laid on the man's shoulder, and he closed his eyes to focus on moving between the realms. With a hard shove, he pushed him from the shadows and right into humanity.

He had seen enough of light and darkness to know this man would be a blight on Zemē and Danye's desire for him to live did not stop Death from dropping him right into the middle of a busy, vehicle heavy street.

The sooner he died, the better off the world would be, but the tainted man escaped death in the first minute. The fae male watched as he rolled out of harm's way, half in one realm, half in another, battling the feeling that he would not see this soul again until he had ravaged the realm.

A cry echoed from the shadows, a feral roll of vengeance from the back of his throat. It was instantly recognisable as primal, male, and utterly fae. Death spun before Danye could make any judgement. He leapt into the shadows before the gorgon could invite this evil into the realms.

His scythe sliced through the air swiftly. The fae male grunted, caught unawares. The shadows in his eyes dimmed, and his body fell to two pieces. He cleaved the male in half. Death stared down at the body, unfeeling and unrepentant. An unnecessary shell.

"What was that for?!" Danye hissed. Outrage was clear in the hiss of her voice. "He could have been fun to play with!"

Death turned a face of cold fury on the demoness and for the first time since he come into his power, Danye shrank in the face of what she saw there. The shadows wreathed him, embodied him, and when Death spoke again, his inner demons echoed in the words.

"No dark fae shall live."

Death would never allow his position in fae society, his rejection from his brethren, his misfortune to be the experience of another. He swiftly collected the soul, ended before it could begin, and cradled it in his hand. This soul would head into the Triplean Fields, eventually. He would not allow it a rebirth, in case fate offered it the same form again.

Danye huffed, and it rolled off her forked tongue as a soft hiss. "Get out then."

"Excuse me?" Death's face tightened with annoyance.

"If you're going to take the fun out of it all, you may leave." Danye hissed. "I'll call you back for the souls when I'm done."

Death grit his teeth, prepared to argue.

The gorgon hissed, before her gaze turned to the next demon, a shadowy imp that emerged from the rift. Effectively dismissing him with the diversion of her attention.

"Go, Death. You're no longer needed." Danye waved her clawed hand. "You overstepped and now I will let every evil thing that comes next out into your precious realms, and you will learn your lessons by cleaning up after them for centuries to come."

Death growled, but the world spun, and he slammed back into Iriya as Danye evicted him from her realm.

Shadow-walker or not, she could keep him out.

He stood, dusting himself off and dropping his scythe to the floor. It clattered loudly, and he kicked it beneath the bed, frustration roiling through him. He emptied the bag of soul encasing opal spheres into a large glass bowl for his trip to the crossroads. No less than a thousand ready for judgement, but he kept that of shadowed fae in his palm, clenched tight, unable to escape him.

Death sighed heavily. He went to the basin, gripping the edges and leaning over it. When he looked up, he could see blood, flesh and shadow-burns making his skin. His black eyes glowed with energy, the demon within burning to get out. His palm ached with the tight grip he held on the fae's soul.

There was a bowl in his bathroom, filled with a mixture of opal orbs and rough-cut pieces of the gem. He took the orb holding the fae and dropped it in among them, hidden with the three others shadowed fae he had taken during his reign. One day, he would give them peace, but not that day, not until the end of his time.

When he glanced back at the mirror, he noticed the shadow developing in the corner, and twisted to meet it head on. Jael took form in the middle of the room, arms folded across his chest.

"Busy week," Jael commented.

Death nodded his head at the glass bowl of spheres.

Jael grunted as he counted them. "So, few."

"Danye kicked me out," he admitted.

"Why?"

Death's gaze darkened, and Jael's expression turned grave. "Another one?"

The angels knew he didn't allow shadow fae to be born, that he wanted no new version of himself across the four realms, but that didn't mean he wanted to talk about it.

"I'm going out... to Solis and Zemē," Death pushed his sleeves to his elbows and reached for the scythe again. "Prepare Yael. We judge on my return."

"You're leaving like that?" Jael asked. "Covered in shadow muck and demon-knows what else?"

He stared at Jael for a second, his black eyes glowing with barely suppressed rage. At the shadows, at Danye, at himself. He shook his head.

"I am Death. Who cares what I look like? Nobody sees me anyway."

15

Death took his time to appear in Quaver court. Keziah had waited long after they retrieved the body. Keziah had learned that she didn't much like waiting. Princesses, even second princesses, weren't used to delayed gratification and so the longer Death took, the more agitated she became. She paced along the halls, twisting strands of her hair between her fingers into tangles as she waited, and waited, and waited. Cursing him more with each hour to pass.

She had hoped he could arrive before they discovered the dead girl, but Juliette's shriek of horror was a sound that would never leave her memory, nor the devastated sobs that rolled from her chest, high and keening in their desperation as she begged the girl to live.

It was in that moment that Keziah realised that the serving girl had been her favoured maid's daughter.

Guilt flickered in her belly at the sight of Juliette's pain, it reflected in the tremble of her murderess hands, but she pushed it away and followed quietly as they lifted the girl's body onto a stretcher and carried her down the stairs to the rooms below the castle.

She followed them, a ghost, lying in wait.

He still did not come after the bustle of grieving servants had disappeared for their beds and other responsibilities. Juliette had stilled as sleep claimed her, cradling her daughter's body, as if she couldn't bear to let her go. Her breathing settled into an even pace as emotion gave way to exhaustion.

In the quiet moments after her cries settled, he arrived. He moved within the shadows of the castle, passing through the walls as if the world did not exist for him; one moment Keziah stood beside Juliette, staring into the still face of her daughter and seeing more similarities than ever before, and the next he stood across the body from her, the lights flickering low in his presence.

Keziah startled when her gaze drifted and found him there. Splattered by what looked to be black ink and smelling like he had crawled out of the gutter.

"Make a noise, next time!" Keziah demanded stridently.

Death's dark eyes narrowed, a deadly edge lacing his voice. "Next time?"

Keziah swallowed, even as her heart sung—he could see her! Simultaneously, her chest ached with worry that she might say the wrong thing and he could disappear. "I..."

His attention turned to the body, and she felt a flare of anger that he wasn't engaging with her. A soft sigh rolled heavily from her lips, knowing she was not his priority.

She should have felt guilty that she had murdered a girl to bring him here, but her relief numbed everything else. It had worked, and he was here. Covered in a strange black gunk, but here all the same.

"You can see me," Keziah stated the obvious.

Dark eyes threatened to set her ablaze. Death's lips pressed into a thin line. "And you me."

"That's…" Keziah trailed off as she tried to find her nerve. Her soft dandelion spine would be useless against this male. He didn't invite conversation, he didn't invite her presence at all. It would sweep her away and she would become lost in the wind if she didn't find her nerve. "That's not what I meant."

Death blinked slowly. "What did you mean?"

"Nobody else can see me. Only you." Keziah whispered. "I'm powerless and invisible in this castle."

His slender, pale nostrils flared as if he was scenting for a lie. The grim twist of his lips tilted upwards. Just a fraction, the breath before a smile, which died before it could form properly.

"You are a princess in one of the high courts of Solis," he told her dismissively. "You are not invisible; you have never been invisible. Princess, you have power.

Keziah frowned. "You—"

"If you are unseen, princess, it is because you choose to be. You are the only person in your way."

"That's not true!"

"Is it not?" He asked blandly. "Or are you ignorant?"

"Nobody would choose this!" Keziah hissed, bells jingling as she stamped her foot, a petulant child in the face of a god. "Nobody would want to live as I do!"

Light flickered in Death's dark gaze, tension cording in his jaw. "This girl would have given half the world to live like you."

The sweep of his hand drew her attention back to Juliette's daughter, but still the guilt did not come.

"So?" She challenged.

Death scowled. "You're a Quaver? Born to be compelling, no?"

"I'm..." Keziah's chest felt like it was deflating. Her stubbornness fracturing. "I'm a second princess."

"And?" Death did not care for her excuses, or the politics of the sirens.

"We don't get even a fraction of the power, and..." The male was frowning at her, his face turned cloudy.

"Hmm."

"Hmm, what?!" Keziah

"Nothing," Death shifted then, rolling his strong shoulders and refocussing on the body laid between them. "Leave."

"No," Keziah argued. "I don't think I will."

His temper flared across his face, shadows rolling across his skin, before he asked, "Did you know this girl?"

"Yes," The lie was acrid and poisonous on her tongue.

"Did you know her well?"

"Uh..." Keziah's breath caught in her chest as Death leaned forward. His hand reached for the girl's chest, and desperately she tried to distract him and prolong his presence.

"What happened to you?" Keziah asked.

Death paused, fingers pressed against the serving girl's chest, his hand looked too big, too otherworldly, against her death paled skin. His jaw clenched with frustration. He spared Keziah only a second of an irritated glance.

"Death happened."

"What?" She didn't understand.

His pale hand sunk into the girl's chest. It slipped through easily flesh and bone, and Death pushed past the mortal shell of the girl and reached for her soul. It stubbornly lingered, a life cut too short, but Death closed his eyes and coaxed her free.

Keziah's gasp shattered the silence.

Death cradled the silver essence between his slender fingers. His eyes snapped open, dark gaze settled on Keziah, so intense that she took a step back, sliding behind Juliette's sleeping form as if the woman could act as a shield.

Death slipped the silvery piece of soul into a jewelled sphere. Keziah watched it disappear, nervously avoiding the anger that flared in his gaze.

"You killed her," Death hissed.

Keziah lifted her chin and pursed her lips to stop words from spilling out. It had been a statement and not a question and she refused to beg for his forgiveness, not from the male who stole souls.

Death pulled himself to his full height. Tall, lithe, intimidating. He advanced closer to her, dark and dangerous.

Keziah, in turn, planted her hands on the curve of her hips. Still, she did not answer.

"Why?" He demanded.

"I wanted to see you," She admitted.

Triumph flared through the siren at the surprise that sprawled across his features. His nostrils flared before Death gained control of himself.

"You're despicable."

Keziah inhaled sharply. "Excuse you?!"

"You heard me," Death held tight to that gem with the soul inside, and Keziah fleetingly wondered what would happen if she were to take it from him. "You took a life just to glimpse something you don't even understand. You're a foolish little girl playing dangerous games."

"So?" There was a strident edge to her tone.

"Do you know her name?" He asked, face clouded.

"Uhhh..."

"It's Lyra." Death hissed. "Do you know what killing innocents does to you?"

Death had rounded the table now, advancing on her quickly. For every step he moved forward, Keziah slipped backwards until cold stone crowded her on one side, and angry male on the other.

Keziah shook her head.

"Do you know what as mark that puts on your soul?"

She stared up at him, breath coming shorter at his proximity. He was so close that the stench on his body overwhelmed her, and Keziah had to breathe through her mouth.

"No," she whispered.

"Do you know," Death growled. "What it does to her?"

Keziah looked to where he pointed, to Juliette who still slept soundly beside her daughter's dead body. Somewhere, deep inside Keziah's chest, it felt like her heart skipped a beat with regret.

"She'll be okay..." It felt like as disappointing answer, one she wished she could take back the moment it left her lips, because surely Juliette would grieve forever.

Death growled ferally again, his fist slammed into the wall beside Keziah's head. The stone fractured beneath his knuckles, hinting that he had more strength than she'd guessed. The siren flinched, curling smaller beneath the fury of his gaze.

"I see every moment, birth to death, when I take a soul. I am the final judge of an entire life. That female will never recover, and it will colour everything in her life. You have ruined her!"

Keziah trembled as she met his glare. "Why are you telling me this?"

Death's fists uncurled; his palms laid flat against the stone beside her head as he stared down at Keziah. The sigh that heaved from his chest was heavy, and weighted. She felt like he was disappointed in her, although she had no idea what unspoken rule she had broken.

"I'm telling you so that you understand what you did!"

"I know what I did," Keziah whispered, tilting her face up to him. "I called you, Death. I called you and you came to me."

Death glared. "Foolish girl."

A feral growl of warning vibrated in the back of his throat. His breath brushed over her cheek, and Keziah closed her eyes, heart hammering in her ears as she took a second to revel in how close he stood.

He was gone before she could process it, his whisper lingering in the shell of her ear. "Don't do it again."

16

The crossroads lay empty, the silence lingering in all directions now that the souls had departed to their new destinies. Death stretched slowly and groaned as tight muscles bunched in his shoulders and back.

"Perhaps," Yael appeared from nowhere. "You need a holiday."

Death raised a brow, his lips thinned as he regarded Yael in all her light and glory, they resembled one of the souls that he had released today, a birdlike girl from Zemē, soft and innocent, taking from life too soon.

"Where exactly do you expect me to go?" He indulged her ridiculous theory.

"Most go places they've never been, or places they loved the most, Grim."

He shook his head and pushed long hair from his gaze, scraping it back into a ponytail and securing it with a strap from around his wrist. "I am Death, I have been everywhere."

"So? Pick your favourite place." Yael floated closer as they turned towards Varelle City. A city of polished opal and eternal quiet, the home he had carved for himself and rarely spent time inside. He had a dining hall, an office, a ballroom, bed chambers and used very few of them. There were rooms he had never even seen, left to gather dust in his absence.

Death did not sleep, not in the thousands of years since he had fallen into his position. Sometimes he wished he were his predecessor, human and bound only for thirty years in this role, instead of doomed to live out the average Fae lifetime.

Yael laughed. "You can't tell me that's your favourite place in four realms."

"No," he snapped, too quickly.

"Where then, Grim?"

Death was silent. They walked back towards the palace in the distance, a cloud of shadows still lingered above the entire realm, not as tumultuous as they had been, but grey enough to remind him of a certain siren.

"In Solis," he admitted finally. "Within the Ash Court there is a place I loved to visit as a youngling. The Grove of Asiah."

Yael's glow brightened. "Tell me more."

"It is a place of solace, where the border of the Ash Fae meets the territory of the Freshwater Mer. It has rivers so clear you can see the stones and sand on the bottom, count the fish if you wanted. The Mer there are so happy that you relax in their presence, on grass so soft you can sleep for hours. When I was young—" Death caught himself.

The silence grew between them, but Yael was wise enough to wait him out.

His teeth clenched, eyes closed, and he scoffed from the back of his throat. "Why do you always do this?"

"Do what?" Yael sounded too innocent.

"Make me think of the past," He rounded on Yael, angel of light, with rage simmering in his blood. "I left the Fae a long time ago. They exiled me. You encouraged me to stay here. Why make me think of them, of things I can't have?"

Yael clucked her tongue, a soft, pitying noise that did nothing more than leave Death more irritated. "Because, Grim, it's been fifteen hundred years and you've never been back there. You were fae before you were Death, and you will be fae in your next life again, don't hate them all for how that elder treated you."

Death scoffed. "Bullshit."

They turned the corner into Varelle City, souls from the Triplean Fields wandered down the road, quiet and peaceful in their chatter, but when Death approached, they shifted to other business, clearing a path.

His throat turned tight, dark gaze swinging onto Yael. "I'm not wanted there," He stated. "Elder Raahn, the old bastard, made that as clear as the river in the Grove of Asiah."

"His misconceptions should not be your beliefs, Grim."

Death's nose flared. He turned away, glancing over the fields in front of his home, littered with blooming blood-red poppies. The splash of colour a stark contrast to the black and grey of his realm, one bloomed for every soul he returned home.

"Grim?" Yael caught his attention, hovering in the boarder to the city.

"What?" He growled.

"Go home," Yael murmured. "Look in on Elder Raahn and remind yourself..."

"Of what exactly?"

"That you have grown, Grim, despite your darkness. That he is the one who lost for shunning you."

Death and Yael were both so silent that the whistle of the winds across the planes of Varelle sung a haunting tune. Every fibre of him revolted against the concept of going back to the Ash Court and facing those who had been a part of his former life.

"I am not wanted there," He repeated firmly.

"Then where are you wanted?" Yael pressed. "Here?"

They both knew the truth, even the souls did not want Death here. They did not seek him out or welcome his presence, he was a trauma remembered.

"I don't know," He forced the words over stiff lips.

"With Danye?" Yael pressed.

"Not always," Death admitted. "No."

"Then where? Where are you wanted, Grim?"

He said nothing but thought of a siren princess with blood on her hands, scarring her soul just for the chance of an audience with him. He thought of the way her face had lit up when she realised that he was standing there, the heat that had burned in her sea-storm eyes when he pressed close, the soft compliance in her body when he caged her in.

Death swallowed roughly.

"I belong nowhere, Yael. That is my curse to bear."

17

Three days before her sister's curse of invisibility lifted and one week before the coronation celebrations began, Keziah killed again.

During yet another grand dinner, as sirens from all three courts vied for the hand of the Quaver queen, the female in the throne on her left sipped idly from a sweet, bubbly drink.

The glass slipped from Queen Silene's fingers and crashed against the floor; the goblet rolled down the steps of the dais. Keziah watched from behind the throne as liquid splattered across the floor, soaking poison laced wine into the carpets.

The Queen of the Dreamous Court gasped for air, her body twitching and trembling as the poison worked its way through her system. Her eyes rolled back, body thrashing in the throne as the other queens and their heirs' screams tore through the room.

Chaos ensued. Vilianne scrambled towards the thrones, terror written across her face and reaching for her mother, when a guard caught her around the waist and swung her backwards.

The guards pulled Queens' Kalani and Elvira from their thrones, herded of the room in search of a safety. Everyone else scrambled to save themselves and as a result, Queen Silene of Dreamous died alone, with only Keziah watching on as she took her last breath and the light dulled in her eyes.

When the first few brave souls returned to the hall, Quinn's broken wail pierced through the room at the sight of her dead adopted mother.

For the first time Keziah's stomach twisted with the smallest amount of regret. This time murder hadn't just been an impulsive action she could blame on her overwhelming emotions, she had not pushed a girl down the stairs on an afterthought. No, she had thought this move long and hard, she had worked out what the best poison was to use, and how to slip it in Queen Silene's favourite wine.

Death had implied she did have power, and it was her own limitations that left her useless, words that had stewed in her mind for days and days on end.

Keziah had decided that he was her power; she could bring death to Solis. Even if her compulsion wore thin, grew as feeble as her song was without the influence of the moon. There was power in being able to see him, she would sing to Death with her actions rather than her words.

The tome on un-innocuous concoctions was a thin book in the Head Healer's personal library, the ingredients scattered throughout the kitchen and gardens. She had studied the poison at length before replacing the tome, so the blame would fall on the healer or his apprentice and not herself.

It had taken time for Keziah to work out exactly how to brew it, and even as she had slipped the concoction into the carafe of bubbling, sweet siren wine she hadn't been sure it would work. She had half convinced herself it would only give the queen a stomach-ache.

Quinn broke free of her guard and stumbled into the cavernous space left around the poisoned queen, where not even the remnant of her guard dared approach.

Keziah barely slipped out of the way as her friend slammed into her mother's body. Her hands clasped against the queen's cold, dead cheeks, pain distorting her features.

"Mama!?" She whispered. Keziah knelt softly on the dais as she watched her friend come undone. "Mama!? Wake up?! Someone go! Get the healer! Get him now!"

Whispers rippled across the court, nobility liked nothing more than a scandal, and they bowed their heads, murmuring sweet stories to one another. Within a day the story of Queen Seline's murder would have spread right across Solis.

Vilianne peered out from behind her guards, skin shimmering as she absorbed more power, true proof of her mother's passing; she was ascending to her position as Queen of Dreamous as they waited.

The guards allowed nobody to leave the room as the healer marched inside, his case dragged noisily along behind him. His apprentice hovered three steps behind.

The Healer knelt beside the queen. He was a carnality siren with little power who had moved to Quaver for his wife, a fair skinned woman of little power, who had wanted to be near her people. His moustache was thick and bristly, and every time Keziah saw it, she wondered how it didn't make him sneeze.

Now, as it twitched with each scrunch of his nose, she loathed it. Especially as he peered at the edges of the dead queen's lips, peeled her eyelids back to look at her pupils, and quietly inspected her nail beds.

"Poison," he declared.

Half the court gasped. "It's an assassination!"

"Two dead queens in as many months!"

"Are we even safe here?!"

"Who's doing this?" The court was lit with questions, suspicion thrown in all directions. "Who's killing our queens?"

Keziah stood slowly, brushing her hands down the front of her skirts. She had removed all her bells for this moment, and in three days when she reappeared to the world, she would put them back on, but for now she waited, safe in the invisibility her sister had granted.

She waited for Death to come.

18

Danye arched her back, her scaled skin gleaming with a soft sheen of sweat in the flickering light of the bar.

Dark nails scratched deeply into his chest, drawing blood as the gorgon rolled her hips and groaned, grinding her hips to slide deeper on Death's thick cock.

He bought forgiveness with orgasms. Three days of fucking without so much as pausing for air. He had wrung them out of her, making her count each one as she came, smirking as the number grew.

Death gripped her hips tightly, pulling the demon queen closer, thrusting his hips up to drive deeper inside her wet cunt.

Her breath hitched on a hiss as he bottomed out, and he smirked triumphantly.

"Again." She demanded, claws digging deeper.

Death obliged and thrust his hips up. They fucked on the bar top. He lay against the wood, her muscular legs wrapped over him, and he rose to meet every roll of her hips, sliding hard into her until she moaned. Fuck, he loved it when she moaned.

Danye shifted, unbalancing them both, and they rolled, crashing down onto the floor. Death pressed his body over hers, his lips sliding along the column of her neck, nipping at the sensitive point by her collarbone. The snakes coiled in her hair hissed with pleasure.

"You good?" He murmured.

"You better not stop," Danye growled back.

"I wasn't planning to..." He gripped her hips, flipping the gorgon onto her stomach and covering her body with his own, pressed skin to scale. His hard, slick cock rubbed against the curve of her arse as Danye pushed back against him, teasing him.

Death growled from the back of his throat.

His teeth grazed the junction where her neck met her throat. Danye squirmed. "Hurry."

"Hmm," Death chuckled. "I'll savour it if I want to..."

He didn't make her wait. The gorgon hissed sharply as Death slid into her, burying his cock, inch by inch, until they pressed flush together, the weight of him pinning her to the floor.

"Move," Dayne demanded.

Death rocked his hips, just a fraction, just enough to feel her clench around his throbbing cock. A primal hiss rolled from her body, and he slid his hands along her soft scales.

"More!"

He eased himself out of her, slowly dragging himself backwards, running his mouth along the curve of her spine as he shifted.

"What did you say?"

"I said more!" Danye hissed loudly, lifting off the floor to follow him.

"Uh, uh, uh," Death swatted her arse before pressing a palm against her back, pushing her down against the rigid wooden floors. He lifted her hips with the other hand, ready and waiting. He kissed the curve of her arse, finding the sensitive flesh at the curve where her thigh began. His fingers trailed over her wet heat. "Do you want to come again, Danye?"

"Fuck, yes."

His finger circled the tight bud of her arsehole, massaging gently. Danye groaned in response.

"What's the magic word?" He taunted.

"You bastard." The gorgon and her snakes hissed. Death straightened, stroking her hips, her spine, those gleaming scales impossibly soft beneath his hands.

"That's not it," He teased, pressing close. She wriggled against him, and his fingers moved to find the bundle of nerves between her thighs, circling lazily.

"Hurry!"

"Not that either." His fingers pressed a touch harder, and she bucked her hips, forcing friction trying to take what she wanted from him. Danye's back arched. A groan rolled from her throat.

"Death..."

"Yes, Danye?"

"Fuck me," she hissed. "Or fuck off."

"As you wish, my Demon Queen." Death smiled. All the pressure disappeared from her throbbing clit as he leaned back, putting space between them.

Not a single part of him touched her, and wreathed in shadows, he made no sound, as if he had simply disappeared. Dayne's resounding growl of frustration rattled the bottles lining the bar.

He chuckled, a dark and sensual sound, and snatched at her hips, thrusting hard to bury himself deep inside her. A scream rolled from the back of Danye's throat. His grip tightened on her hips, pulling her backwards as he thrust hard.

"Yes," she hissed. "Yes, Death! Yesssss! Right there! Don't you fucking stop!"

She tightened around him, shivers working down her spine as all the muscles in her body locked up. Death kept moving, thrusting into her repeatedly, until his body coiled, too, on the edge of pleasure.

He laced his fingers around her neck, squeezing tight as he groaned, restricting her air until spots danced in her vision. He took her close to death as they both barrelled towards orgasm.

Danye's body shuddered around him as she hissed loudly. She squeezed tight, milking his cock.

Death tossed his head back, a growl rolling from deep inside his chest, and faltered... All the pleasure building in his body evaporated in an instant.

"Yael?" He spluttered, shocked.

"Yael?!" Danye roared, "What the fuck?!"

Before he could stop her, the demon queen, in all her naked glory, peeled herself from beneath him, and launched herself at the Angel of Light, fangs bared and sharp claws looking for purchase.

Yael slipped easily out of the way of the spitting serpent, hissing as her claws caught their leg.

The angel of light regarded him gravely as they shifted out of reach. "Holiday's over, Grim."

"Grim?" Danye hissed. Spinning on him, she was a picture of naked fury. "That's your name?!"

"No!" Death scrubbed a hand over his face, reaching for his pants but taking his time to cover himself. "Why are you here, Yael?"

"There are souls to collect."

"And?" He growled. "There are always souls to collect. You couldn't wait for me to—"

"—Finish?" Danye supplied, reaching over the bar for a corked bottle and flicking it open with one black nail.

Yael giggled, and Death narrowed his eyes.

The Demon Queen wriggled her body back into her dress and drank from the bottle. "You know, if Yael had ever been fucked, she'd have more respect for pleasure."

The angel of light scoffed. "It's important."

Death sighed. "Isn't it always?"

"Well..."

"You're the one that told me to take time off." Death told her, taking a dirty rag to the blood that ran down his chest and managing only to smudge it across his chest.

Yael's eyes narrowed on the bite marks lining his skin, dotted in the pattern of Danye's fangs. Her light dimmed. "This isn't exactly what I meant."

Danye scoffed and walked to the door, wine bottle swinging in her hand. She didn't bother with goodbyes as she kicked open the door and moved back into her realm.

"Tell me," Death turned back to Yael. Frustration tight across his features. "What's so important that you had to interrupt?"

"The Queen of Dreamous has been murdered."

19

Death was three days late in collecting the soul of Queen Seline of Dreamous. A set of investigators from the Ash Fae had arrived before he turned up. Keziah had returned to the view of the sirens before he came, and her movements became bound by the watchful eyes within the castle. Everyone was suspicious and on edge in the wake of a murder.

As the days wore on, she worried she had missed him completely, that Death had come and go from Quaver Castle without giving her so much as a second thought. The idea of it left her anxious, the bells at her ankles jingling as she tapped her heel impatiently.

She had a connection with Death. She knew it to be true. More than the fact that he came when she called, more than the fact that she could see him when everyone else's eyes slipped right past him, there was something else there that she couldn't quite name.

It had to do with the way her blood heated when he was nearby, the thrill she felt when too close to him. Keziah wanted nothing more than to drown herself in his dark gaze, and fight to make that look of disapproval become a begrudging smile. She wanted Death to notice her, and for everyday that he did not come, she plummeted further and further into a bad mood.

"Keziah," Juliette approached the restless princess, soft hands redirecting her to sit in the chair. Juliette had aged a decade in the weeks since her daughter had died. "I know you're scared, but they're going to find out who did this. The Ash Fae investigators are the best in Solis, steady and impartial, dedicated to the truth."

Everyone had taken her anxiety as fear for her own life, and Keziah didn't bother to correct it. Instead, she huffed, hands fluttering around her stomach. She couldn't work out what to say and started pacing again.

She would never see Death now, confined to her rooms for her own safety, now that everyone could see her again. When she twisted again, the siren turned her best pout on her maid. "Can we go for a walk?"

Juliette looked nervous. "I don't know, Princess."

"I just..." She tipped her head back, staring at the ceiling as tears prickled in her eyes. Frustration and disappointment, so certain that she had missed his visit. "I want to go see Quinn. Make sure she's okay."

Juliette's eyes flickered to the guard who stood solemn and quiet just by the door. He shook his head.

Keziah burst into tears to sway them. It wasn't hard, with so much pent-up emotion. "Please?"

She didn't want to miss him, to have gone to so much trouble to draw him here, to see him again and now ridiculous rules would keep them apart. The air felt too thin in her lungs, her clothing too tight against her skin, and Keziah anchored her hands in her hair, repeating, "Please?!"

"It's for your own safety, Princess," the guard from the door called softly. "Until the fae inquisition settles, nobody leaves their quarters."

Tears fell freely from her eyes, and the siren sniffled. Juliette pressed against her, wrapping her arms firmly around Keziah in a tight hug. "Quinn is grieving, but she will be okay. I promise you." Her voice held the broken edge of someone who knew grief.

Keziah nodded against Juliette's chest; she'd already known that. For the past three nights, Quinn had drawn herself and Thea into dreams where she raged and sobbed in equal measure. She had been there for her friend, holding her tight, and wondering why she didn't feel worse for the trauma she'd caused.

"I just want to—"

"Shh," Juliette stroked her curls softly. "I know."

"No, you don't." Keziah whispered, crying for herself and all she missed. Salty, selfish tears. "Nobody understands but him."

Death loomed over Keziah when she opened her eyes. She lay beneath the heavy duvet, where Juliette had tucked her in with the whispered advice to sleep, and

Keziah hadn't been able to stop herself from following the advice.

His face was tight with anger, and his eyes reflected the storms of another world, shadowed and dangerous. There was a cold judgement in his features.

"You're here!" Keziah shot upright, and Death's hand wrapped around her throat, pushing her back against the sheets. The squeeze of his fingers cut off her next words.

"Be still," He hissed. "And tell me why you killed the Queen?"

She struggled to inhale beneath his grip around her windpipe. Her fingers scrabbled against his hand, nails biting into his skin. Death relaxed his grip enough for her to cough.

"I didn't," Keziah gasped, and shoved at him, struggling to sit up. Her legs kicked at the covers, freeing herself from them as best she could.

Between one breath and the next, he had rolled her, trapping her beneath the confines of her own blanket. Straddled over her body in the middle of the bed. His solid thighs braced on either side of her hips and when Keziah's breath hitched, it wasn't because of his grip on her throat.

Death glared down at her, but Keziah could think of nothing except the way his muscled thighs pressed against her sides. Her cheeks flamed red and shamelessly she tried to lift her hips.

"Don't lie to me, princess."

"I'm not," she lied, again.

"I told you I see every moment from birth to death... I've seen the late Dreamous Queen's soul."

"And?"

"Keziah!" He snapped. "Tell me the truth!"

She liked the way he said her name. It was a caress and curse word all in one.

"It was a murder. The queen wouldn't have known who killed her!" Keziah argued. She wriggled to free herself from the confines of the blanket. She ached to touch him, and he was so close, if only she could get herself free. He was acknowledging her in a way that nobody else did. "You can't tell me that a glimpse into the last moments of her life showed my face."

Death leaned close. There was a cold fury written in his face, a murderous rage of his own. His hair fell over his shoulders and tickled her nose.

"Who else would want to kill her?" He asked.

Keziah's face scrunched as his hair brushed against her again, a featherlight touch, and then violently sneezed.

"Achoo!" Spittle flew at him.

Death flinched backwards, horror morphing across his features as he raised a hand to wipe flecks of her saliva off his face.

Keziah wanted to die, completely mortified, but even then, she couldn't escape him. The most dangerously attractive male of her life was straddling her body. He was hers alone since nobody else could see him, and she had sneezed into his face.

"Sorry," she muttered.

Death pinched at the bridge of his nose with long fingers. "You are the bane of my existence, little siren."

As much as she tried to suppress it, Keziah smiled, taking the acknowledgement that he at least thought of her enough to have decided she annoyed him.

"I'm right though," Keziah drew his attention back to her, wanting to prolong the moment. "You can't tell who killed the queen."

"No," Death admitted through grit teeth.

"It could have been anyone," Keziah continued. "Queens have many enemies. But after you saw her, you came to see me."

He grunted.

"Did you miss me?" Keziah asked daringly.

Death huffed and rolled off the princess. He rubbed a hand across his face and paced the length of the bed.

"What are you doing, Keziah?"

She struggled out from beneath the blanket, kicking it off. "I like the way you say my name."

Death glared as if he wanted to poison her himself. "You shouldn't."

"But I do," she whispered. "You see me. I want that. I want..."

He drew close again, and Keziah held her breath, looking up at him, hoping he would close the gap further. She closed her eyes, preparing herself for the possibility that he could kiss her, but when she looked up, Death had stepped back and carefully put space between them.

"You should forget me."

"No."

"Why?" he growled. "I don't want you, Keziah of Quaver."

She flinched; his words hurt. "You don't mean that."

"Yes, I do! You're just a little girl, playing games you don't understand."

"I'm not a little girl!" Keziah drew herself to her full height and closed the gap between them. She gathered her nerve. "I'll prove it to you. Stay with me."

Death did not move, he did not speak. He stared at her with those fathomless eyes until Keziah shrunk away, cowed by the silent rejection.

"Juvenile," He murmured then. "Because an adult would know better."

Keziah's eyes dropped to the floor. "I just wanted..."

"I know what you wanted," Death growled. "You're as subtle as a brick to the face."

She blushed. "I..."

He turned to walk away, without another word, without so much as a goodbye. Desperation flickered in her belly, a spark to ignite a flame of frustration fuelled anger and Keziah drew herself to her full height. She searched deep within herself for the drops of magic she knew she had.

He was right; she was a Quaver Princess and compelling others was in her birthright, in her blood.

"*Stop*," Keziah sung.

Much to her shock, Death stopped. He stood still, and Keziah swallowed roughly. A bead of sweat dripped down her spine, fingertips tingling with panic that pooled as dread in the pit of her stomach.

"*You will not leave.*" She could feel the magic in her voice, feel the shimmer of power just beneath her dark skin, a glow that formed within. "*You will stay with me.*"

Death rotated slowly on the spot, breaking through the bonds of her magic. He moved swiftly towards her, a cat stalking a mouse. Instinct had Keziah backing until her thighs hit the bed and she dropped into the soft cushions.

His knee slipped between her legs, pressed against the apex of her thighs, his long body blanketing her own until his blank face lingered a fraction from her own. Keziah could feel every one of his exhales brushing against her lips. If she lifted her head, just slightly, she could kiss him.

She tried to move, but his long fingers anchored in the curls of her hair, pinning her in place as Death dropped the blank mask to reveal the war that raged across his face.

"Is this what you wanted?" He whispered.

"Yes," Keziah whimpered back. Unable to help herself.

"Three times now you have tried to control me, princess." There was a sharp warning in his tone. It sent a shiver through her body. "I am Death, born of the Sholheim Rift. Nobody controls me."

She whimpered, fear like ice on her skin when the whites of his eyes disappeared, all the heat she felt from his body blanketing her own disappeared. Shadows curled up his neck, his body grew cold, his face changing beneath the darkness.

"But..."

"Be careful what you wish for, Princess. Try to influence me again and I will stay with you." He warned, as Keziah inhaled sharply. "Then I will break you into a thousand irreparable pieces."

He disappeared, gone in the blink of an eye.

Tears brimmed in her eyes and the conflicting ache of desire in her body burned brighter than it ever had.

Keziah wanted nothing more than to play with Death, to know exactly how he wanted to break her apart.

20

"What do you mean their life cycle ended?" Death spluttered indignantly into the blue flames that crackled in the hearth. "There's still another sixteen shadow years left before I needed to collect them!"

"Well," Danye's reflection hissed, distorted within the dancing flames. "I'm afraid to say you can't do math for shit, Grim. They're due now, so come get them."

"Don't call me that!"

"I like it," Danye cackled. "You're stuck with it, Grim."

Her face slipped out of view as she turned to someone or something beside her, the snakes in her hair writhing angrily. When Danye turned back to their conversation, her face was tight with anger. "Just come quickly, Grim, I need their souls gone before the Oni hatchlings eat them."

He groaned and glanced down at the plate of food at his dining table, now cold. His stomach rumbled a protest and Death grit his teeth. He strode through the polished halls and out onto the balcony that overlooked the sea of red poppies.

"Jael!" Death called into the night.

The angel of darkness materialised by his side. "Why must you always call me here? Why not visit the Underground? Visit me instead. We'll tour the caverns."

Death frowned. "The Shadow-Wraiths are coming."

Jael's responding groan could have shaken the earth. "Again?!"

"Indeed."

He huffed loudly. "I swear their last life cycle only ended a week ago. Such is the passage of time here."

Death nodded abruptly. "Just remember—"

"I know, I know," Jael interrupted. "You can't capture wraith souls. I've been doing this longer than you, Grim. Complete chaos is coming."

Death turned back inside, catching sight of his weary reflection. At the mirror he paused, frowning at the sight of himself, confused why the little siren had wanted his attention so badly.

Luckily, all been quiet in Solis for weeks now. She seemed to have calmed her murderous tendencies. He shook off the thought of Keziah and reached for his scythe. Duty called.

Souls poured into Iriya through the tear he had created between the two realms. Wraith-souls, notoriously mischievous in both life and in death, notoriously slippery demons even after their lives ended. So hard to catch that Death had stopped trying and merely shepherded them through the tear in the realms, until they landed in Varelle, frenzied and destructive.

He had had no help from the Demon Queen to collect them. She was busy preparing for new hatchlings, reorganising her realm. After Death herded them to re-birth, the wraiths would hatch again in Kihnes, the same souls living in cycles of mischief.

When they reached Iriya, the wraith-souls destroyed everything within reach. Death followed once he had shepherded the last soul through and stared at the remnants of his city.

Varelle itself did not just comprise his home, built into the side of the mountain, but shops, houses, and a winding marketplace. Each one petitioned for by the souls, through Yael. Cherry picking the best parts of their previous lives. He had never denied them a request in their peaceful afterlife.

Those who had chosen the everlasting rest of the Triplean Fields had tangibility and full reign across Iriya to make their lives as they wanted it, with only the one rule they did not take the Solitary Walk and nor cross into the Oplean Underground. Death simply created what they needed and left them to it. A strange but peaceful society.

As per usual, the wraiths decimated it with ease. He walked down the opal paved streets and picked up overturned chairs. Shattered ceramic crunched underfoot.

He picked up a painting, a torn canvas that had once depicted the field of poppies, and set it against the shop. He sighed heavily. It would take a lot of energy, and time, to rebuild.

They had ravaged the path to his home, the wild poppy fields trampled, and in the distance, the door of his palace ripped free of the hinges. It lay discarded on the ground. He could only imagine the havoc the souls had wreaked inside, unafraid of repercussions.

Death rubbed at his face and considered that he may be too old to keep dealing with these situations, but the face of Death did not retire, he expired.

A low whine pierced through the field on his left, halting his movement. He paused and twisted, peering into the darkness. Often, he walked these streets alone, souls darting out of the way, so the presence of another left him on edge.

Death clenched his fists and shadows burst from his fingers, curling around his wrists and up to his elbows. "Come out here."

Another low whine, but nobody approached. The issue with herding wraith-souls through the tear, and mending it afterwards, meant other monsters slipped through too, and he tensed in wait to see what monster had come to Iriya.

"I won't ask again," He growled, voice dangerously low.

Shadows slipped through a nearby building, dissipating and reappearing in front of him. Shifting and flickering into the shape of a small hound.

Death stared down at it. His nose flared, frustrated at yet another task on his list. He would have to deliver it back to Danye.

"Fall through, did you?"

The hound rolled onto its back, presenting its belly with a whine. Death rubbed at the back of his neck. If he were to go to Kihnes now, the remaining wraiths would level the entire Iriya before he returned, and if they destroyed the structure of the Underground, the worst of souls would roam free. It would cause more trouble than it was worth.

"You can wait," Death told the hound. "I have things to do."

The hound rolled back onto its stomach, crouched low, regarding him curiously but did not whine again. Happy enough with the response, Death walked off, his scythe in hand as he searched for the last of the wraiths within the city.

The hound followed.

He paused, mid-step, and sighed. "Go away."

The hound sat.

"I mean it," Death said.

The hound didn't move, and every time he did, it slunk after him, staying close to his heels.

Fifty minutes later, Death had an ache in his jaw from how hard he clenched his teeth. The hound just would not go away.

"Three more left and then I'm taking you back and dumping you in Danye's bar," he told the hound, trying to relax enough to detect the wraith-souls, a harder feat in Iriya where souls lingered in every crevice, hiding from both him and the wraiths.

The hound whined in protest, and Death ignored it.

When the shadow-hound spotted one wraith, before Death could stop it, it let out a yip, darting ahead and racing around the soft light of the soul. By the time Death approached, it had herded the wraith into a small corner and yipped proudly.

He blinked. "Well done."

The hound preened beneath his praise.

"I'm still not keeping you," He warned.

He felt Yael and Jael appear behind him in the street. Yael asked, "Almost done, Grim?"

"Two more after this one, I think, and then it's another season complete."

"Who's the mutt?" Jael questioned.

The shadow-hound growled, taking offense.

"Don't know, don't care, but it's rounding them up." He clicked his fingers sharply and the shadow-hound looked back at him, the ice of its gaze piercing. "Chase it to the solitary walk. Chase it all the way into the river."

He pointed towards said river. The hound yipped and its shadowy form flickered, but it turned to the soul, and chased it far away.

Death turned back to the angels. Jael stood, against a wall with his arms folded across his chest. Yael was coaxing a squashed red, poppy to stand tall again without much success.

"You should name it," Jael suggested, and he groaned.

"I'm not keeping it!"

"Shadow?" Jael continued as if he hadn't spoken.

Yael snorted softly. "Too on the nose."

"Soul-killer?"

Death narrowed his eyes on him. "You two have caused me fifteen centuries of pain. Why I would I adopt a third entity to live here and annoy me for eternity?"

Both were silent as they contemplated his words.

"Because you're lonely," Yael murmured.

"I am not!"

The hound raced a circle around them, yipping loudly, chasing the final two wraith-souls down the Solitary Walk. Death watched solemnly as all three disappeared into the fog that rolled the river, silently hoping the shadow-hound would fall into the water and be reborn to save him a trip to another realm.

"Call it Sgàil," Yael said.

Death blinked. "Snail!?"

Yael's light glowed as if she were laughing at him. "Sgàil." A soft correction. "It means shadow, but it's less obvious."

Death shook his head. "We're not keeping it."

"Sure, we are," Jael grinned, all slightly pointed teeth.

"We—" The hound was there again, sitting happily at his feet, flaming blue eyes peering up at him. Death looked down at it, the most pitiful shadow-hound he had ever seen and realised he had already lost this fight.

"Fine," He hissed.

The angels laughed with frightening synchronicity.

"But you're both feeding it. Not me."

They laughed again, the sound following Death as he strode towards his broken front door.

"Come on then, Sgàil."

21

The fae inquisition arrived at Quaver Court at the behest of the three Siren Queens, two young and one old, the latter of which feared that she would lose her life next. She stated she didn't feel safe in the castle with a murderer on the loose, but also feared returning home in case the culprit was among one of her own.

They arrived as a party of five, led by the oldest fae male that Keziah had ever seen, albeit if she hadn't seen too many fae males in her lifetime.

The three solemn queens held full court for their arrival, and so she stood, dressed up and quiet to the left of Queen

Kalani as the Ash Fae males strode into the hall and bowed low.

"Rise," Queen Kalani murmured. Not a song, but a sign of protocol, and everyone relaxed at those words as much as they could under the circumstances.

The four tall males behind the old fae were young and slightly familiar. Keziah realised she could see the resemblance to Death in their high cheekbones, pointed ears, and firm chins. Although, they all had a quiet confidence, a stark difference to the disdainful expression Death usually wore when he looked in her direction. While they appeared bored and harmless, a threat lingered in the air, the implication that these males were deadly.

The old man straightened slowly. "Queens, Kalani, Elvira and Vilianne, we thank you for inviting us and wish to express our regrets that such sad circumstances are the reason for this meeting of siren and fae."

The three queens smiled back stiffly. Keziah watched her sister out of the corner of her eye, waiting to see if she would try to exert any of her power over this old man. She didn't. Her sister merely nodded and motioned for him to continue.

"I am Elder Raahn, of the Ash City. May I present the four chosen princes of Ash. Niall, Master of Air—" One of the Fae men stepped forward and bowed low. He was slender, tall and his yellow blonde hair sat in every direction.

"Fionn, Master of Water—" Dark haired and dark eyed, Fionn didn't bother to smile as he swept low and straightened, stepping back into the line.

"Cillian, Master of Fire..." This was the biggest of the four princes. His dark hair curled at the nape of his neck, a fraction longer than the others. He kept his eyes on Queen Kalani as he bowed and stared longer as he stepped back into the line.

"Tadhg, Master of Earth..." Tadhg grinned widely as he stepped forward, impish in his appearance. He bowed quickly before settling back in place behind their Elder.

Keziah watched them all carefully. The Ash Fae were renowned for their attempts to be fair, logical, and educated. For this reason, the Sirens used them to mediate on problems that they could not solve themselves. Usually, this was ownership disputes between the three courts and their desire for certain pieces of land. Never in her memory had the Ash Fae come for murder, and Keziah wasn't sure how their elemental powers could help them weasel out the truth.

She was certain that she would take the secret to her grave.

"Tell us what you need, Elder Raahn," Queen Elvira stated. "I am keen to put this matter to rest."

The old fae smiled, a grim look on his aged face. "Nobody comes or goes from this castle until our work is complete. We will interview everyone within these walls and report back to you with our findings."

"You will find justice for Silene?" Elvira leaned forward, fingers curled around the armrests of her throne, her eyes narrowed on the five fae males as if she suspected them, too.

"The truth always has a way of coming to light, my queens." Elder Raahn stated calmly.

Keziah shrunk back against the side of the throne as he said this, because for a heart stopping moment, it felt like he was looking right into her soul.

The interviews began and took a dreadfully long time. Keziah waited with Quinn and Thea, day after day, for her turn, but it never seemed to come. With every passing day, she spun a new lie to her friends, explaining away the days she had been unseen, apologising for her absence when Quinn had needed her most. It caused a rift between them that Keziah wasn't entirely sure how to fix.

They lay beneath the soft morning light in the conservatory, staring at the glitter of dust particles trapped in the sun as it shone through the glass roof.

"Was it worth it?" Thea asked with a sigh.

"Hmm?" Keziah turned her head to the side, puzzled.

"Sneaking out to see him," Thea rolled onto her stomach, resting her chin in her palms, and grinning widely. "How scandalous! Princess Keziah of Quaver, out in the village tumbling her passing fae traveller between the common folk's bedsheets."

Keziah giggled, a high, and bright sound filled with nerves. It was too high pitched, but neither of her friends seemed to notice. She closed her eyes and pretended that her story was real, that Death had taken her that night on the bed. Pushed up her skirts, slid his powerful hands up her thighs, and followed the path with his mouth. She imagined he was a man of few words because he had far better use for his tongue.

"She's blushing!" Thea crowed, nudging Quinn. "It must have been good."

Quinn said nothing. She had been quiet and sad since her mother's passing. It was only when she looked at Quinn, in the solemn moments, that Keziah realised what Death had meant when he said he said the loss one would taint the rest of the actions of another. The second princess, now heir, of Dreamous, would never be the same.

"Let's talk about something else..."

"Yes, ladies..." a silky-smooth voice had Keziah bolting upright. "We're bored. Let's talk about something else."

Three of the four Fae princes stalked into the room. They moved with fluid, almost predatory grace, and Keziah could not help but watch whenever they entered a room.

The quiet self-confidence they displayed filled her with an inexplicable jealousy. Keziah wished she could be like that.

"Niall, Fionn, Cillian..." Thea murmured their names in a throaty voice, causing Keziah to give her a wide-eyed look. The Fae Princes were attractive. They had most of all three courts chasing their tails, but Keziah could not forget that they were still here to catch a murderer and she was the one with blood staining her hands. They were, effectively, her enemy.

"So, what were we doing?" Cillian dropped onto the side of the lounge where Keziah lay, and without asking permission, he stretched himself across it. His body nudging against hers.

She raised a dark brow at him. "Relaxing, but you're in my space now."

"Well then," the arrogant fae princeling tapped two fingers his chest and spread his arms. "Lay on top of me."

Keziah hesitated; nerves had formed a knot in her stomach. Thea poked her softly in the side, and she took the encouragement to stretch out against him, kicking off her slippers before she rested her legs across his and tried to relax. She could feel the thrum of his heart through his chest.

Thea was chatting animatedly to Fionn, and Quinn mostly ignored their brother when he sat cross-legged by her side.

"Happy now?" Keziah asked.

"Slightly better," Cillian laughed, a low and husky sound. He broke the lingering silence easily. "Are we the first fae you've met?"

"No," she answered unthinkingly. "I've met a fae before."

"Oh," Cillian sounded curious. "What's their name? Maybe I know them."

"You wouldn't."

"Oh, you're a little liar," He teased, long fingers tickling her ribs and Keziah squirmed away from him, nearly falling off the chaise. "You don't know any fae."

"Of course I do," She huffed, jamming her elbow against his ribs. "I just don't know his name."

She thought that calling him Death would be a little ominous, and she had never given her friend's a name for him, so this princeling didn't deserve one either. Plus, Death felt more like a moniker than a true name.

"What's he look like, then? We've been alive a long time, we likely know your rogue fae."

"Even if he's Argent?" Keziah challenged.

Cillian lifted one thick, dark brow an arrogant smile twisting across his lips. "Even then."

She shook her head and settled back against his chest. "Don't you lot have a job to do?"

"Maybe we're already doing it..."

Keziah frowned. "What?"

"We could be interrogating you, right now," Cillian explained. "What do you think?"

Her heart seemed to lodge itself firmly in her throat, a thrill of fear lighting all her nerve endings on fire. She squirmed against Cillian. Then she caught herself, forcing herself to relax. "No, you're not."

Cillian laughed, but he didn't confirm or deny.

"I've been watching you four," Keziah continued. "You don't question anyone, you just party and flirt. The old man does all the interviewing. You're just here for an enjoyable time."

Cillian's fingers splayed against her ribs, thumb stroking against the exposed skin between her skirt and top. He was quiet.

"Murder is never a good time," Cillian corrected.

Keziah bit down on her lip and forced herself not to protest the statement. If he thought that much, he must never have felt the breathless moment of power when the light dulled from someone's eyes, or the undeniable thrill of knowing that nobody knew what you did.

Half an hour later, she made an excuse to leave, and avoided the fae princelings for the rest of the day. Keziah burned with curiosity though, dying to know if they did know of her deadly fae friend. Or if Death was hers and hers alone.

22

Sirens bustled through the courtyard, fluttering this way and that. Not even one of them noticed him standing by the fountain. Death didn't know why he was there, standing in one of the grand courtyards of Quaver Castle, listening to the way the water splashed, and counting the gold pieces lost to the depths of the fountain on the tail end of a wish.

He wondered what the grey-eyed siren wished for at that fountain, what the intricacies of her desires would be.

There were no souls waiting for collection, although many called to him from Zemē, who still battled through the devastation of their pandemic. But he had been restless in Iriya, pacing the halls, unable to even pretend to sleep and then he had shifted from one realm to another, seeking distraction.

He had not entirely expected to arrive in Solis, but his mind led him here all the same. In the late evening, the castle was still bustling with sirens, and not even one of them could see him, none of them due to die. They simply frolicked among one another, creatures of pleasure.

A tiny child passed through him completely, giggling as they staggered on unsteady feet, as if drunk, and haphazardly launched a coin towards the water. It bounced off the edge and hit the ground with a dull thud. A laughing mother followed the child, and Death flinched as she too walked through him, stooping to collect the coin, and let the infant siren have another attempt. This time, it hit the water with a soft splash.

He backed away then, turning his gaze to the castle and wrestling with the idea to visit the Princess' bedroom again. There would be only one reason that his distraction would lead him to Solis, and that was a frustrating, annoying siren princess.

Death knew he was making a mistake, but he still swept up the steps of the castle and began his search for Keziah.

She was not at dinner, where her sister, the queen, talked animatedly to various males, attention now shared with the new Queen Vilianne. Men who wanted to charm the most powerful women in Solis and become King Consorts, getting their own seat of power in the matriarch-based power system. The father of the next heir would always be powerful, even in a society that valued their females more than their males.

Keziah's bedchambers were empty too, and he stood there, looking at the indent her head had made on the pillow as if he could simply wish her into existence the same way he willed himself to become visible, free of the shadows.

His hands fisted by his sides as he inspected her belongings, the room of luxury that she called her own, and tried to work out what made Keziah special enough to see him when the rest of the realms could not.

She did not appear, and he didn't wait long before marching through the walls in search of her insolent grey gaze. He would pick a fight for his own entertainment, accuse her of the murder he thought she had committed to watch her squirm in front of him.

Instead, he found the little siren in the parlour. An old siren song echoed from a small, lit orb in the corner, imbued with enough magic that it encouraged all who heard it to dance.

Death stepped back towards the wall and called forth the shadows under his control, using them to hide in the corner, protect him from the siren magic in the room, hoping that this extra layer of protection would hide him from Keziah as well.

All because the little siren princess was not alone.

Keziah danced in a wide circle around through the middle of the room, a bottle of wine swinging from her fingertips, head tipped back, infectious laughter on her lips. Her two little friends accompanied her, the second princesses of Dreamous and Carnality, both as lively as Keziah. Unfamiliar women danced around them, close but not too close. Never quite touching them.

His attention turned to the three males and expecting sirens, his blood ran cold at the familiar sight of Cillian, Fionn, Tadhg, and Niall. They danced close to the siren princesses, their hands sliding to guide the sway of their hips, fingers brushing against their skin teasingly.

Death's jaw ached; teeth grit tight as he watched Cillian's fingers glide across Keziah's exposed stomach. She giggled at his touch, twisting in time to the music, the bells on her ankles and wrists jingling softly as she spun again, wriggling herself against him.

Keziah turned in another spin, lifting the bottle to her lips, the glaze of drink hazy in her sea-storm eyes. For a breathtaking second her attention flickered to the corner, and Death inhaled sharply, waiting for her to confront him, to see him, but the shadows and her dulled senses hid him well, skating across his skin and keeping him in the dark.

Cillian recaptured her attention before she could glance back to him again, coaxing her closer, until her lips brushed against his cheek.

Disappointment felt unfamiliar and uncomfortable as it crested through him. He felt tense, wound tight and liable to snap. Even so, he couldn't look away, could not leave the siren alone.

The night wore on, and their dancing became sloppy. Keziah ground against the fae princeling, her arms wound around his neck, her face bright as she beamed up at him with drink-induced confidence.

They wound up pressed against the wall, too close to Death for comfort. She arched her back, pressed against Cillian as he cradled her against the wall, her leg wrapped high around his hip.

"Tell me about your fae friend?" Cillian asked as he tweaked her nipple and she gasped.

Death stilled, hardly breathing as Keziah giggled, her wine bright eyes caught on Cillian and never leaving him.

"What?" She murmured.

"Tell me," Cillian asked again, his lips trailing a path down her neck and across her collarbone as his hand pushed her skirts higher and higher, revealing more of her soft thighs. "What does he look like?"

"He's tall…" Keziah breathed. "And broody, he always looks as if the world has upset him. He has long white hair and eyes like…" She faltered, eyes fluttering as Cillian's fingers found the right spot to make her moan.

"Eyes like what?" He pressed.

Death couldn't help but watch as Cillian's hand disappeared beneath the skirts bunched around Keziah's waist, as he drew another soft moan from her lips. At least until she arched her back, rolling her hips, grinding against Cillian's hand, and his next breath caught painfully in his chest.

His cock strained against his pants, and Death fisted his hands by his sides to restrain from touching himself, from alleviating the tension. He couldn't look away though as Keziah's body rolled, fingers twisting into Cillian's shirt, a breathless moan caught in her throat.

"Like…" The words trailed into a groan. Her head tipped back against the wall, dark curls sticking to her forehead, her eyes half-closed as she shivered with pleasure.

Cillian's hand stopped moving, and Keziah whined with frustration. Her dark lashes fluttered, and she opened her eyes, grey, glazed, and wild as she stared at him, accusingly.

"Keep going!"

"Eyes like what?" His lips traced her neck again, and the little siren melted. "Tell me."

Death's jaw ached, clenched tight, blood hot at the way she rolled her body towards him, wrapping her arms around his neck, melding every inch of her body against his to coax more pleasure from him.

"Like he's seen the beginning and the end of everything," Keziah admitted, gasping as Cillian followed through and began sliding his fingers inside of her again.

"Like he's seen the shadows of everyone..." She added, humming with pleasure, riding his hand, as her fingers trailed down his chest, wrestling with the button that secured the waistband of his pants.

Death sneered as they fell loose, sliding halfway down Cillian's thighs, his pale arse on display. He pressed himself back into the corner of the room, gaze skating to where her breasts heaved with every breath.

He wanted to leave, but he couldn't look away. He wanted to know who the fuck she was talking about and why Cillian, a male from his own past, was asking about it. He wanted to rip her away from him and ask her what the fuck she was thinking, writhing in the arms of an Ash Fae princeling.

Cillian dragged slipped his fingers free, and Keziah whimpered at the loss. He lifted her up easily, despite the soft heaviness of her body, wrapping Keziah's legs around his hips and lining himself up with her core. He wrenched her top up, exposing heavy breasts and hard, pebbled dark nipples, they heaved with her every, gasping breath.

"Who is he? Who's your fae friend?" Cillian growled, palming her arse to find the right grip thrusting hard inside of the siren princess.

Keziah's body bucked at the invasion, her fingers twisting to anchor in his shirt, a single word slipping over her lips as she groaned loudly.

Death blinked; his heart turned to stone at that single, breathless word. Before Cillian could thrust into her again, before she could say anything more, he had shifted from Solis to Varelle City.

Heat and tension warred with him as Death tore off his clothes and fisted his cock, stroking himself hard as he imagined the pliable, wet heat of the manipulative siren princess wrapped around him instead, the way he would fuck her hard, a punishment. All while Keziah's keening, desperate and breathy admission haunted him.

"Death." She had named him. "Death.

23

Keziah felt a bead of sweat roll from her neck and trace a path along her spine. The room was warm, uncomfortably so, and she squirmed in her seat, teeth dragging over her full lower lip again. She fidgeted with her diadem, ensuring it sat straight.

Elder Raahn regarded her from behind half-spectacles that had slipped down the bridge of his nose. He said little, comfortable in the same silence that left Keziah's heart aflutter and filled her with the intense need to shift and talk. She hated the silence as much as she hated waiting and the two combined felt like torture.

A strange concept for an invisible girl. Her fingers twisted in the jewellery at her wrists the tiny bells jingling with each movement, until the noise annoyed her, and she fell still.

"Death," Elder Raahn said softly.

His strange accent pulled at the words, and it sounded like 'dee-ath.' Ash fae believed in their own refinement, education, and neutrality across Solis; and somehow it showed in the way Elder Raahn took his time with everything. The world could simply wait for him to be ready.

Keziah's eyes narrowed and flicked accusingly to Cillian, who stood behind his shoulder, his face impassive. Her head ached, a side effect of too much fae wine, and all she wanted to do was crawl back beneath the heavy covers of her bed and sleep for a week. She hadn't stomached breakfast three hours ago, and now her belly let out a reproachful grumble.

Cillian had had other plans that morning. He had dragged her out of bed with him, playful promises spewing from his soft lips, and Keziah had followed, smiling wide, preening under his attention. It was a special feeling to capture the attention of one of the fae princelings. Enough so that she had ignored her dizziness and the pounding in her head.

Until he had pulled her into one of the East Wing sitting rooms and announced that his Elder wanted to have a little chat. Suddenly, all his playful words had dried up, and he had nothing more to say on the matter. The chasm that opened between them was cold and ghastly.

"You have a friend called—"

"Why is it so hot in here?" Keziah cut Elder Raahn off quickly. "Honestly, it's three-billion degrees."

Cillian's face clouded over at the disrespect to his elder. "Because you're still drink laden and dehydrated, maybe?"

Keziah lifted her chin, glaring at him. "No."

"Because—" Elder Raahn interjected. "Cillian wants it to be, Princess. Nothing more, nothing less."

They lapsed back into uncomfortable silence. Keziah picked at the flecking gold paint on her nails, peeling it free. Her fingers hovered a fraction from her lips, anxiously about to bite at her nails before the magic struck a chord.

An old command of her mothers, princesses did not bite their nails, it was a dirty habit unbefitting of her station.

Keziah had never won over the instinct to chew on her nails when her anxiety spiked, but the magic always prevented her from following through.

Elder Raahn knotted his hands in his lap. He waited until the silence and the heat felt like it was suffocating Keziah, and then he spoke again.

"As I was saying," He murmured. "You have a friend called 'Death'?"

Keziah bit down on her lower lip. "Yes."

"Is that a euphemism?"

She thought about the question, lips pressed firmly together and cheeks colouring as she considered the word he had used. The stares of both Elder Raahn and Cillian left her wanting the floor to open and swallow her whole; neither one moved as they wanted for her answer.

"Uhh," Keziah hesitated.

"Answer the question," Elder Raahn pressed.

"I'm afraid I don't understand what you mean..."

"Is 'Death' a euphemism?"

"Euphemism," Keziah repeated the word slowly, pulling it apart. "You mean like when a male says one thing, but he's actually talking about the size of his di—"

"Princess!" Cillian's growl filled the room, cutting her off. Keziah lifted her gaze to his and held it for one beat of her heart, two, three, before she glanced back down at her hands.

Her sister, Queen Kalani, would have owned the statement, stared them down until they let her finish it. Keziah knew it was one of the many reasons her sister was the firstborn, and the new queen. But Keziah's dandelion spine swayed and came apart in a strong wind, so she stared down at her hands until she needed to break the silence again.

"No."

"Is 'Death' a nickname for the murderer in your court?"

Keziah shook her head quickly, her springy curls bouncing. "He doesn't kill, he..."

It wasn't her story or secret to tell, so Keziah swallowed down the words and lifted her head to stare down the Elder and Princeling.

"If it is," Elder Raahn continued, as if she hadn't spoken. "Then it's very concerning that the Princess of Quaver knows the person who has brutally murdered a queen?"

Keziah pressed her lips together tightly to avoid commenting. She desperately wanted to be seen, but this was not how she wanted it to happen.

"Do you know the murderer?" Elder Raahn asked plainly.

She stayed stubbornly silent.

"Is your friend involved in these murders?"

Keziah pursed her lips.

"Did you ever ask someone to kill the siren queens for you?"

She blinked and broke her silence. "Queens? Multiple?"

Elder Raahn tilted his head. "It is rare for sirens to have short lifespans; you should have been centuries old before your mother died naturally."

Keziah frowned. "But I am..."

"What?" The Elder looked perplexed.

Laughter bubbled up her throat, high pitched and hysterical. "We age as slowly as the Fae. I am only two years younger than Queen Kalani, who will celebrate her two-hundred and fifty-seventh birthday in a few months' time. That would make me two hundred and fifty-five this coming winter."

The fae males exchanged surprised looks.

"I am not infantile," Keziah told him sharply. "And if I was, then your princeling ought to be ashamed of his actions last night."

They both ignored that pointed comment.

"Your birth registration states you are twenty-four years old," Elder Raahn stated, remaining calm in the face of Keziah's strident tone and implications.

"No," Keziah shook her head. "Second princesses are not traditionally registered with the fae. My true birth record does not exist within the Ash Archives. Twenty-four years ago, was when the Argent fae visited Quaver Court. My mother submitted a record of life for me in case we needed to cross their borders with a change of plans, but that was merely a statement that I lived not a declaration of my birth."

Elder Raahn leaned forward, his aged face heavy with agitation. "Impossible. All births, deaths and mating-bonds in Solis must register with us."

"Tell me," Keziah countered. "If you register birth, you must always register the corresponding death?"

"Yes."

"If a death is questionable, just like the murder of the Dreamous queen, the Ash Fae would investigate it?"

"You know this already, Princess."

Keziah clutched at the arms of her chair, fingers curling into the cushioned material as she dug for the will to keep going.

"They dispose of second-born siren princesses of when the first daughter ascends and produces a new heir," she whispered, unable to say it with any strength. "The queens avoid registering us, otherwise each generation would have to report a suspicious death at a time of glorious celebration... What would the Ash Fae think if it just kept happening? If they had records of generational death at the same time as a new birth."

Elder Raahn's face had creased with conflict as he processed this information.

"We would know. If this were happening, we would know. The Ash have lived long before we birthed the Siren race and they crawled from the Mer waters to assume their place on the land."

Keziah inhaled sharply and shook her head; ego existed in all parts of Solis. No amount of fairness and candour could stop ego.

"I'm telling the truth!" She told him firmly.

"You are making up lies," the fae Elder corrected. "I suspect to cover up for what your friend has done."

Frustration felt like a buzzing bee hovering around her chest, riling her up, leaving her wound until Keziah slammed her hands down on the armrests of the chair.

"*Listen to me!*" The words came out soft and lilted, but with the powerful melody of her siren gifts. Keziah's deep, bronzed skin glowed softly as magic settled across the room. She blinked, stunned as the magic settled. Cillian and Elder Raahn watched her carefully, all their attention focused on her within seconds. Her body hummed with power as the magic took hold.

Their eyes flickered to one another, before Cillian dropped his chin. His thick, dark brow lifted. "We're listening."

Keziah leaned forward and cleared her throat softly. Disappointment was bitter when her next words came out tinged with frustration but free of power. "*I am not a child, and I had nothing to do with my mother's death. Your records are wrong.*"

They exchanged another look, the corner of Cillian's full mouth dropping, his chin lifting. Keziah did not know what any of it meant, despite their frustrating brief looks. Her head still ached, and she felt as if she had run a marathon.

Frustration and power left her frazzled, her nerves tingling until she wanted to climb out of her own skin.

"Princess Keziah—"

A knock at the door cut off the next question. Elder Raahn's lips thinned with disapproval, his brows pulled together in a way that left his already thin face looking even more severe.

"Yes." He called.

The door opened and another of the princelings strolled in, Keziah tried to remember his name but drew a blank even as he turned to offer her a wink before murmuring low in his Elder's ear.

Raahn nodded slowly. He rose in a fluid movement, and the invading Princeling ushered him out the door. "Excuse me, Princess."

The old fae paused at the threshold and glanced back over his shoulder at Cillian, who dipped his chin a fraction. When Elder Raahn left, he slipped comfortably into the old male's seat.

Keziah glanced up at him from beneath her lashes, and he employed his mentor's method of interrogation, waiting her out until the silence became unbearable.

She jiggled her foot, tapping her toes, the bells at her ankles ringing as a symphony to her growing anxiety.

"So..." Keziah waved a hand. "I'm going back to bed."

"Nope." Cillian popped the syllable and settled back in the chair. His slender fingers raked through the curling ends of his hair, and he watched Keziah closely. "You stay here."

"Until he comes back?"

"Until we finish talking."

"Well," Keziah offered Cillian a sharp smile. "We have nothing more to discuss. You didn't have to tell him about Death, or any of the other stupid things I said when I was drunk."

Cillian's eyes brightened. "This Death character is a lie, like Raahn said, isn't he?"

"No," Keziah huffed, her face crumpling into a frown. Although she knew she should have agreed with him and pretended the other fae male didn't exist.

"Your friends know about him, so maybe at first it was just a lie to make yourself look good. It would be fun to have a male so interested, a fae, so they'd never wonder why they couldn't meet him. I understand why you might do it, Princess. It can't be easy being friends with Princess Theodosia."

"What do you mean?" Keziah asked sharply, daring him to continue down that path.

"She's a Carnality Princess," Cillian sounded condescending. His eyes rolled, an action that set Keziah on edge. "All eyes are always on Aubrie and Thea when they enter a room. They are sex incarnate, males and females alike lust for them. No man would look your way when Thea dances beside you."

Keziah blushed deeply, her arms folded defensively across her chest and accused, "You did."

"I interrogated you."

"Right." The single word was sharp. "Maybe that's why it was lacklustre sex."

Cillian's face clouded over. His nostrils flared, as if he were struggling to control himself, but then he cleared his throat and continued. "So maybe it starts as a lie to make yourself feel better, pretending there's a male who's looking at you, not Theodosia, and then it evolves and becomes an excuse."

"An excuse for what?" Keziah sniped, although her heart had beat harder, faster, and she prayed the fae male couldn't hear the change in it. He smirked as if he could.

"Murder."

Keziah forced a breathy scoff across her lips. It felt unnatural. "How would I murder someone?"

Cillian leaned forward, bracing his forearms on his knees as he watched Keziah closely. "Isn't it obvious?"

"Obviously not."

"You're a Quaver Siren, the second strongest in all of Solis. You could just command the Dreamous Queen to drink poison straight."

She watched him, unblinking, as her chest squeezed with fear and relief swept through her all at once. Keziah knew in that moment that she would survive the interview; her own incompetence would be her saviour. She laughed, despite herself.

"That's not how it works... the Quaver Songs."

Cillian smirked, "Little liar."

"It would take a lot of power to do that. Influencing another siren queen is no small feat."

"You're a Princess, you're next in line to the Queen's power." Cillian's face turned smug. A distinctly unattractive look on him. "It was you, or Queen Kalani herself, I'm sure of it."

Keziah tried to pick up the fragmented pieces of her self-confidence and strength of will before she admitted, "I don't have that sort of power."

His lips tugged up at the corner, disbelief in his smile. He thought he had caught her out. "Prove it."

"What?!" Keziah spluttered.

"You heard me." Cillian gripped the base of his chair and dragged it closer, so close that their knees touched. Keziah fought not to recoil. Last night she had wanted him to touch her everywhere, but now, on the precipice of discovery, she wanted him nowhere near her.

"You want me to show you I can't use magic on you?"

"Yes."

"But..."

"Exactly!"

Keziah ground her teeth together. "Aren't you princelings supposed to be chosen ones? I thought that came with some level of intelligence."

He arched a brow. "I was intelligent enough for you last night."

"Your intelligence, or lack thereof, has nothing to do with your being a poor fuck."

"You were moaning pretty hard last night, Princess."

She rolled her eyes. "Me displaying my lack of power will be me doing nothing at all, which you'll say is because I'm not trying, not because I can't do it. I can't win, either way."

"Keziah," he said her name silkily, leaning closer.

She hated that she still liked the way he said her name, liked the way he paid attention to her enough to be accusing her at all.

"I know you can't win because Raahn and I just saw and felt your power."

Her hands bunched into fists, nails biting into the fleshy part of her palm. "That was coincidence. Mere chance. I'm a *second* princess. I have no power."

Cillian scoffed. "Tell me to do something."

Keziah's stormy eyes rolled, but she snapped, "Stand up."

He didn't move.

Cillian tilted his head. "Are you even trying?"

"I told you that you would say that!"

He tapped one long finger against his lips, humming beneath his breath. From the look in his eye, she guessed the mystery of her fluxing and pitiful power was a more interesting game than catching a murder to this fae male.

"What did you feel when you did it before?" He asked.

"Frustration," Keziah didn't hesitate in her answer. "I'm talking to two people thicker than a castle wall."

He snorted but didn't argue the point, instead; he nodded as if he had worked out the secrets to the universe.

"Keziah," He murmured.

The heat in the room seemed to triple, Keziah's shirt clung to her back, skin turning slippery with sweat. She knew it was his doing. He was trying to make her uncomfortable.

"What?"

"Use magic."

She scoffed. "Or what? I told you; I can't do it."

"Or I'll drag you by your hair to the throne room. I'll dump you like trash in front of the three queens and tell them it was you. I'll tell them you murdered two queens: a power hungry little sirret who needed a better fix. I'll announce that you're coming for Queen Kalani's crown."

Keziah's mouth had dried out. Her head spun, she could feel the fear in her body as if it were a living, breathing entity clawing its way from her blood.

"I would never..." she whispered.

Her chest felt tight, breaths coming heavier, and her fingers beginning to tremble. All her mother's old curses meant there she couldn't physically attempt to take the crown from Queen Kalani. She couldn't even touch her sister; let alone harm her sister.

Not that it mattered, it only mattered that Kalani would believe him. The tightness in the chest doubled, crushing her lungs, and making it difficult to breathe.

"I..." Keziah spluttered.

Her blood ran hot and cold. There was no telling what her sister would do. Keziah's entire body shook, spots dancing in front of her eyes. She fisted her hands in her dark curls and buried her hands in her lap.

Kalani was going to kill her. In front of everyone, she would be known as a traitor. The powerless Princess desperate for more. Keziah's stomach had twisted into a tangled mess of knots.

Cillian smirked widely. "I'll tell them—"

"*Stop.*" Keziah demanded; voice high pitched with wild panic, she buried her head in her hands, fisting her fingers in her dark curls as she screeched at him. *"Just... Stop talking, stop breathing, just stop everything and shut up for a moment!"*

Despite the garbled fear in the command, power flowed through it. Keziah could feel the essence of her song swelling in her chest, filling every breath she took. The magic left her invigorated and alive, she basked in the glow of it. The thrill of magic was like snorting crushed saltwater merscale only better.

It took time, but Keziah's breathing evened out, and the elation drowned out the panic that she had felt, the strength that burned in her blood and bone from the use of her power. The heat of the room seemed to dissipate. She basked in it, a wild laugh bubbling from her chest, and she drew a deep breath, finally feeling like herself again.

When Keziah of Quaver pulled the frayed edges of herself together and tossed her head back, straightening to meet the arrogant gaze of the princeling. She had enough courage to see this through, to face his quipped remarks and arrogant smile.

At the sight of him, her heart skipped a beat, turned to stone, and plummeted to her stomach.

Cillian lay slumped in the chair, pale skinned with a blue tinge to his lips, all the life in his eyes had flickered out, dull and vacant as they stared back.

"Oh fuck,' Keziah reached for him, shaking his shoulder, but he didn't move. Her fingers pressed against his neck, just above a purple mark she had made with her mouth the night before, and she tried to find his pulse.

Nothing.

Keziah swallowed, her entire body trembling as she recalled telling him to stop breathing to get him to stop. The magic, *her magic*, had worked.

"Shit, shit, shit." Keziah stumbled to her feet, skirting away from the dead princeling, and backing towards the door.

There would be no denying this crime, having been the last person in the room with him, even if it were the only accidental death so far.

Keziah stared back at the dead fae, her heart squeezing with a mixture of fear and anticipation. She needed to hide, hide away until a saviour came, because Death was coming for Cillian of the Ash Fae. Accidental or purposeful death, it didn't matter, Death would show up to collect his soul, of that Keziah was sure.

When he arrived, she would ask him to save her, too.

24

An eerie silence had fallen over Quaver Castle, and it left a chill in even Death's bones as he strolled through the opulent halls. Trouble was brewing in Solis, and this latest murder would unsettle everything.

Losing two Siren Queens and now a Fae Prince in the space of a few short months would create turmoil across the land. The hierarchies of power would tip, as the fae were an ancient race with an ancient memory and they would not forget this treachery.

Death knew he would visit Solis more often in the years to come, a frustration since the long lives of magic users meant he spent more time with the humans and less in the lands of his past. These changes would be taxing.

He turned a corner, brushing past the right curtains, and came to an abrupt halt, hands lifting from his pockets as he took in the man who stood resolutely in the middle of the hall.

Elder Raahn looked as if he had not aged a day in the time since he had last seen him, well over a millennium ago. The old fae stood in his plain brown robes, pointed chin, and hooked nose tilted. Death watched as the old Fae tilted his head a fraction, listening.

"I can't see you," Elder Raahn sounded much the same as he had back then, too. Death clenched his teeth, fighting not to flinch in the face of his elder. "But I can feel you here."

Death stood still, nostrils flaring as he waited out the bluff. He stood in front of an old mentor, the man who had spun stories of the four chosen princelings of power and given a young fae male hope of a place, of power, and then rejected him when the shadows came. His own gift despicable in the eyes of Ash and Argent.

Elder Raahn did not back down. "It is you... Isn't it?"

The silence that echoed between them was as loud as any answer could have been, and Death mused that the old man would look a fool if anyone came looking and saw him muttering to himself.

Death exhaled and moved to step around him. He was here for Cillian, nothing more, nothing less.

"It was something that foolish girl said," Elder Raahn continued steadily. "About her friend having seen the shadows in everyone."

Death stilled, turning slowly to settle his gaze on the man again. Was he talking about Keziah? He folded his arms across his chest, and he waited to hear more.

"Now," Elder Raahn straightened. Death could hear the soft pop and crack of his back as he stretched it. "The only fae male I know who danced with shadows was just a foolish fledgling who disappeared before they could deal with him."

Death's lips thinned.

"He should have killed himself, as I requested, but..." The Elder shook his head and stepped forward. His robes swung at his feet; a smug smirk marred his face. "You're very much here, aren't you—"

"You will not speak my name," Death snapped, his voice harsh in the quiet hall, breaking through the shadow that hid him. "It is not yours to say."

The old fae laughed.

Death's knuckles cracked as he clenched his hands. Shadows rose to the forefront of his soul, slipping over his skin and swirling around his hands like armour.

"Show yourself." Elder Raahn demanded.

Death blew out a slow breath. He stalked to stand right in front of the old fae and willed himself into sight. The layers of shadows that kept his work hidden slipped inside of him and he stood tall in front of his old mentor, sneering down his nose at the old male.

He had grown taller than the fae who had ruled his childhood. A male who had moulded a generation in the shape of the goals of his foolish council. Believing that he had a real, prominent influence on Solis.

Elder Raahn had to look up to scowl at him. "What have you been doing, boy?"

Irritation rolled through Death, and the shadows curled up to his elbows. "What I do is none of your business, old man."

"Until you kill just for a piece of pretty siren," Raahn growled.

Death frowned. What had Keziah told them?

"Dark Fae may not live." Elder Raahn hissed the familiar rhetoric, laced with hatred and fear.

He could have flinched, hearing the same words he had said to Danye voiced back to him, an old belief ingrained in his soul.

Death steeled himself. "Yet, here I am."

"You are not the exception to the rule," Elder Raahn growled. "I will deal with you, boy."

With a shake of his head, Death shifted to pass the old man, but Elder Raahn — ever stubborn — moved into his path again, and again. A ball of water formed at his fingertips; derision set into his thin, lined face. Tension coiled in his body as he shifted into a well-known offensive stance.

"Move," Death commanded.

Raahn stood tall and stubborn. "You will be reprimanded for your crimes, boy, and the consequence is death."

Death growled, but the sound rolled into a breathless laugh. It echoed hauntingly down the halls.

"I am Death, old man," He advanced so sharply that the old Fae took a step back. "I am the gatekeeper of the Iriya, where death thrives. Move aside, I am not here for you. It is not your time to die."

Death sneered at him, reaching to his back, and unsheathing his scythe. The handle carved of the glittering black, Iriya opals, flashing with colour beneath the light in the hall, the sharp blade thin and deadly. He wished it were Raahn's time to die, wished he could cleave his soul from his remains.

"You admit it then," Elder Raahn shifted, and before Death could inhale, the elder blasted him with a ball of water. The force of it sent him staggering back a few steps. "You're a murderer, and this is the confession of your crimes."

A low growl rolled from the back of Death's throat, growing in intensity until the lantern fixtures rattled along the hall. He straightened; the hard shake of his head sent droplets of water flying in every direction.

"Water was always the weakest of the elements," Death mused. "As I grew, I wished for the hot destruction of fire like Cillian or even earth. At least that would be useful. Are you going to drown me, old man?

Swiftly, he closed the gap between them until he towered over his old mentor.

"No," Elder Raahn looked unfazed, his upper lip curling back to flash sharp canines. "I'll simply evaporate all the water in your body. Killing you will be easy, boy."

Death laughed again, a haunting sound. "Killing me is not as easy as you think. I've tried."

"Everyone dies."

"Not the Attoria. Not the soul collector." He growled.

Elder Raahn flinched.

Death had different names in diverse cultures, and he had heard the stories growing up. Among the fae, the spirits of Attoria took the most deserving of fae souls to a place of eternal rest. They prettied up the stories of Death and his Iriya to suit their own desires of what came next. Through the realms, he honoured the cultures and traditions of what each believed the time after death to be, and when he visited the Fae courts, he banished most shadows to create the appearance of more light, and he took the bodies with him, disintegrating flesh and bone in the shadows, so that the fae could continue to believe that their Attoria had taken the entire male or female to their resting place.

He was not so cruel as to shatter their beliefs.

"The Attoria are pure," Raahn snarled. "Not tainted with darkness like you."

Death reached for the old fae, shadows dancing at his hands, and Elder Raahn skittered out of reach. There was a familiar fear flickering in his eyes, tightening across his face. Most people feared death, in one way or another, but Elder Raahn had always feared the Dark Fae more, feared the disruptive evil that he believed they represented.

Death watched as the old man moved his hand in familiar conjuring motions, the twist of his wrist a move that every Ash Fae learned as a child. But predictably, he felt nothing.

Death would not perish at his hand.

"Believe what you want," he said finally. "But I am here for Cillian."

Elder Raahn's body jerked at the sound of the princelings name. He bared his teeth in threat, tensing as he crouched in a low, defensive position. Primal instinct to defend a loved one.

"I don't need magic; I'll rip your throat out with my teeth."

He sighed, but the old fae didn't let up. Elder Raahn leapt forward, slammed into Death, and both went rolling to the floor with a loud thump.

The scythe clattered on the ground as Elder Raahn swung his fists, and Death moved to catch them.

A growl of predatory warning echoed down the hall when Raahn found purchase and his fist slammed into Death's cheek hard enough to knock his skull into the stone floor with a sharp crack.

He had known this soul would be trouble to collect. There hadn't been a princeling death in his entire career and now Death regretted doing his duty at all, if only for the headache it caused him.

Dark eyes narrowed on his old mentor, and with a roar, he shoved him back, sending him flying until he slammed into the wall. The old fae crumpled, but much to Death's surprise, he found the energy to rise again.

Elder Raahn doused him in water, forcing it down his throat until Death's lungs burned and he fell to his knees. Long enough for the old man to find his feet again.

Death coughed water and spit onto the floor. Tension coiled in his body as he rose slowly to his feet, cold fury twisted across his face. He pushed his long, wet hair from his face and advanced.

As he moved, he held out his hand, the gleaming scythe lifting from the ground and flying into his grip.

Death swung it idly in an arc; and the sound of the blade slicing through the air cut between them. Elder Raahn's gaze focussed so intently on the sharp edge that when Death shifted again, he missed the sweep of the handle.

It slammed into the old fae's legs, cutting him off at the knees, and he crumpled to the ground. Quick and driven, Death was on top of him before he could move, knee pressing hard into the elder's chest, the blade of his scythe twisted to the old man's throat.

"It's not your time," Death growled. "But I could make an exception."

He smiled widely, baring his sharp teeth in threat as Death shifted his weight, pressing down with his knee until he heard the crack of breaking ribs.

The old man gasped in pain.

"I am here for Cillian," Death repeated slowly. "Don't stand in my way, or you will go with him, and you both have very different fates awaiting you in my realm."

The old Fae, eyes as blue as river water and now marred with pain, stared up at him. "Don't take him."

"Not your choice."

"Let..." Elder Raahn gasped again. "Let me take him home. I must offer him to the Attoria properly."

"I am the Attoria!" Death roared in his face.

The edge of his scythe shifted, grazing the man's throat, and drawing a thin line of crimson against his skin. "Me and me alone, for a Solisan millennium!"

"No!" Elder Raahn gasped. "Do right by him. He was your brother, once."

Death flinched, but Elder Raahn was not wrong. Cillian had been in the same generation as him, raised in the same stone courtyards and attending the same lessons, waiting for proof of where they belonged. But Cillian developed his fire at an early age, and become a favoured son, whereas Death had waited in the shadows for his moment to come, only to find rejection from their elders.

"This is right for him."

"It's not! You'll damn him! You won't have any part of him to feed into your shadows, you demon!

Death pressed harder against his chest, and Elder Raahn fell silent, wheezing for breath against the weight on his lungs.

"If I don't take his soul, he will remain here. Untethered and unrested. He will never have another chance."

Elder Raahn spat, and it landed on Death's cheek. The ultimate disrespect. "Do not touch him."

Death stared down at him impassively. It was hard to resist the impulse to cleave the life from Raahn Lelheir, who had already lived many lifetimes, to peel his soul from his mortal shell and leave him in the underground to rot. Solis, he thought, would be a better place without his vile man.

"*Fine*," Death growled. "Keep his soul."

He was on his feet, looming above the old man. Shadows and darkness swirled around him as Death shook his head, water dripping to the floor.

"But remember this old man," He spat. "When the Attoria does not come, for his soul, or any other in your Ash Court—for I will not visit the Ash while you have power—Know that it is your fault. Remember that you doomed them all."

Elder Raahn clutched at his chest, still gasping for air. Death stared down at him and offered himself one more moment to consider the idea of ending his life. The temptation skittered through him, his fingers tightening around the scythe, but he was not, and never had been, a murderer.

Death lifted his chin, staring down the hall in the direction of Cillian's body, and the soul within that cried out for him, begging for release from the horror of death and decay of the body it had left behind.

He pushed a breath through pursed lips and stepped back. Cillian's soul would suffer needlessly, but he would allow it, just to teach Elder Raahn a lesson.

Elder Raahn was old and influential among the fae, but even he could not escape the consequences of his actions.

Nobody had that much power.

Death stepped back again, he twirled the scythe absently, smirking when the old man flinched. His eyes flicked down the hall again, tempted to find the little siren princess who had started all this trouble.

She had told Cillian, and by extension Raahn about him, alerted the fae to the fact that he still lived, and he knew when the Elder returned home, he would spin a story of evil and horror. It was better not to linger.

Death ignored the call of the weeping soul and shifted through the realms in search of his home.

25

There was a quiet edge to dread, and the acidic feeling that pooled in Keziah's heart, and with every beat, pulsed through her veins. Hidden away, she waited and waited, listening to the whispers from servants as they searched for her under the Fae elder's command. Keziah had never wanted to be truly invisible before, not until that moment, as she fretted about the repercussions of her actions.

At first the darkness had been welcome, as she pressed into one of the thin passages the servants used to scuttle about the castle in a hurry.

It didn't last long. The weight of darkness felt suffocating, and Keziah had never been good at sitting still and waiting.

Then, she realised that if she hid in the dark, she would never find Death.

He would come and go without her seeing him. So, Keziah stumbled through the dark tunnels and stairwells used by the castle staff until she could orientate herself and find where they were keeping Cillian's body.

It was hard to get close. The three remaining Princelings stood guard at his door, their expression warped with anger and grief. Vines cracked through the floor; tiny white flowers bloomed at their feet, creating a soft field in the hallway.

Keziah hesitated behind the heavy tapestry, her fingers pressed against the rough fibres and the musty smell overwhelming her senses.

There she waited, watching for the first sign of Death in his approach. She knew he would glide past them, unseen, but she would see him. She always saw him, and she knew how it felt to have people look straight past you, straight through.

That was why she had decided that Death's exasperation at her presence, the frustration that coloured every word, was just a misplaced emotion, discomfort that she truly saw in him.

Everyone wanted acknowledgement, she thought, even him.

From behind the tapestry, the siren princess practiced what she was going to say. There was no use in trying to use her power, even though Keziah so wanted to do it, it never affected Death in the way she wanted.

Now that she controlled a princeling, though, she felt unstoppable. The warm, satiated feeling of using her power still pulsed around her body, lighting her up from the inside out.

Death had no patience for her power. So Keziah would simply have to reason with him. Explain that he should take her with him because she saw him, because it was nothing more than kismet. A siren who could see Death, and Death who himself seemed to see through her façade and see who she really was, too.

There was nothing left for her in Quaver Court, with charges looming and beyond that, only waiting for the end of her usefulness. There was no other option but to go with Death, and Keziah was sure that she could be useful, that he would accept. If he didn't find her interesting, if he didn't want to talk to her, then she was sure that Death would have never engaged with her at all. He could have pretended, like so many others, that she just didn't exist.

Time wore on, and Keziah became increasingly restless. The heady high of using her powers waned, and so her attention turned to the three remaining princes who stood in silent vigil by the door, solemnly guarding their brother's body.

Keziah watched them closely. They didn't speak; they didn't move. She had, somehow, exerted her power on an Ash Prince, when in the past she hadn't been able to convince Juliette to ignore her in the halls so she could slip out to a party in the woods.

The difference, she realised now, had been emotion. Any time that Keziah used wild, potent magic had been during a time of overwhelming emotion.

She thought back through her conversations with Death and his stubborn insistence that she had power, when Keziah had thought all along that she didn't have a drop to spare.

"You are the only thing standing in your way," she repeated his words, turning them over in her mind and trying to prize them apart, like popping seeds free of a pomegranate.

She knew she could do magic without the help of the High Moon now; it had happened once; it could happen again. Keziah just didn't know how to access it, how she had found her magic in that moment of fear and made Cillian of Ash simply stop breathing, stop living.

Her attention turned to Tadhg, the princeling standing closest to her hiding place. He stared at the ground, fists clenched and a vein popping his in forehead. His sharp jaw shifted, and Keziah realised he was grinding his teeth. Beyond that, he was so still that he could be as dead as Cillian.

"Move," the princess whispered.

Nothing happened.

She frowned, letting the tapestry fall back between them, cutting off the light from the hall. In the dark she twisted her hands together and closed her eyes, trying to settle the way her mind raced and the nerves that roiled in her belly.

There had to be a way to access her power. It was there, inside of her somewhere. Keziah swallowed, squinting through the darkness at the chipped polish at the end of her nails, luminescent and gold.

"You can do this, Kez," she whispered to herself. "You have power. You can sing. You can make him do anything you want. Anything at all."

She closed her eyes, drawing in three deep breaths to settle the way her nerves seemed to jitter. She pushed against the rough back of the tapestry and peered out at the fae males again.

"Move."

Nothing. Frustration welled inside of her, hot and mixed with embarrassment that she was as much of a failure as her mother had always foretold.

"*Just move!*"

All three princes stepped forward, alarm flashing across their faces after the action was complete. They exchanged a dark look.

"Come out, come out, Keziah," Fionn called, tension rippling through his body, mirrored in the actions of his brothers as they searched the space for where she hid.

Keziah peered through the crack of light between the stone wall and the tapestry, observing them. Her skin glowed bronzed and she trembled with power.

Tadhg, Niall and Fionn shifted into a triangular formation, steadily creeping down the hall, flattening the soft white flowers beneath their boots.

"Where are you, Keziah?" Tadhg called, his accent thickening the words. "Come out. We just want to talk."

Keziah saw them nod at the tapestry and her heart squeezed tightly in her chest. They were edging towards her panic felt like it would overwhelm her, threatening to send her spiralling. She snatched the tapestry back and burst forward with as much energy as she could muster, slamming into the closest of the fae princelings.

"*Let me through,*" Power reverberated in every word, a melody on her lips. "*You will forge—*"

It was too late, while the princelings had shifted aside and cleared her path to the room and body beyond, she had forgotten entirely about their gifts.

Vines snaked up her ankles, tightly binding her calves until she wobbled to stay upright.

"Goodnight, Princess," Niall crooned and stole the air from her lungs, she gasped, suffocating without oxygen her until shadows curled at the edge of her vision and Keziah's eyes rolled back in her head.

Not one of them moved to catch her as she fell.

26

Storms raged through Iriya, lightening striking the ground. The realm blackened with Death's foul mood. He had not left his palace in days, pacing through the gleaming walls of his self-built cage, and wishing he had taken the opportunity to strike down Raahn when he had the chance.

Jael and Yael hovered in his peripheral vision, glowing balls of light and shadow, waiting for him to offer directives. Their worry grated against his nerves, growing each time he shattered goblets or swung his scythe against the wall.

He knew he was acting like a mere fledgling on the edge of a meltdown, but his emotions demanded to be felt.

"Grim..."

"Leave!"

"But Grim—?"

"I said leave!" He roared, twisting, and launching the scythe at them both. Jael dematerialised, shifting into a ball of slithering darkness just as the sharp edge sailed through him.

Both Jael and Yael blinked out of his view. Death dropped to his knees on the floor shaking with barely suppressed rage. He felt like a fledgling, reliving the humiliation of his rejection from fae society, and the isolation of having to rebuild in Iriya, alone.

Sometime later, as Death sprawled on a new throne of his own making, a bottle of wine in one hand and his scythe gripped in another, scales gleamed in his peripheral vision.

"What are you doing here?" He demanded of Danye.

"Not happy to see me, Grim?"

"I told you not to call me that!"

"Well," The gorgon ducked swiftly as the bottle of wine flew past her head. "We don't always get what we want, Grim."

He bared his teeth, growling, and Danye hissed back. She pushed past his dining table, shoving it out of her way as if it weighed nothing in a simple demonstration of her immense strength, an unsubtle reminder that the demon queen was not a soul to be trifled with. She had reigned for millennia for a reason.

Danye circled Death as he mourned the loss of his wine and glared broodily at the demon. "You're not welcome here."

"Oh, really?"

"Really," Death pushed his body, drink heavy, from the throne and stumbled to his feet. He faced the gorgon and allowed his shadows to roll across his body, consuming him as he stepped into his true form, a creature of pure, reckless, darkness.

Unhidden fear flickered in Danye's eyes as she studied his form, but to her credit she didn't shy away, instead the demoness stepped forward, her clawed hand pressing into his shadows to rest on his chest.

"Tell me, Grim," She murmured, straight faced and serious. "What has your knickers in a knot?"

The absurdity of the question startled him. Death let out a choked noise and banished the shadows, reappearing as an angry fae male.

"You wouldn't understand."

"Try me," Danye challenged, slipping insolently into his throne, and throwing her legs up on the armrest.

He growled in warning, and with a wave of his hand the throne disintegrated beneath her body, melting into the opal floors as if it had never existed.

Danye hit the floor hard but bounced to her feet quickly and stalking into his space.

"Enough!" She hissed. "You promised these souls an eternity of peace and you have broken your word. Not even your pitiful angels can pierce the lack of reason in your thick skull. Your bad temper is not their fault, your lack of reason is not on them. If you cannot control yourself, you do not deserve to control a realm."

Death growled and the realm shook beneath their feet. Beyond his palace, souls shrieked with alarm. Dayne reached for him, as if scolding an errant fledgling, her dark claws piercing his skin.

"It is not their fault."

Death obsessed over her words for days to come; long after he let the storm clouds fade, and through the hours spent trying to reconstruct the buildings he had shattered among the villages forged in the Triplean Fields.

His own palace remained a mess, a reminder of the destruction he had caused.

Danye had been right; it was not the souls or the angels at fault for what he felt. The blame lay securely on himself, and Elder Raahn. There was one other, though, that Death identified as the key source for him torment.

A little siren princess who had been spreading lies about him, whispering his name in the ears of the fae, she was the reason that Raahn had known he would come.

Without her the confrontation would never have happened. Over time he convinced himself that less and less of the blame lay heavy on his shoulders and instead belonged to the siren with the dark skin, springy curls, and sea storm eyes. She who hunted him through worlds and thought she could bring him forth at her disposal.

The more he considered it, the angrier he became with Keziah of Quaver. She needed to be taught a lesson.

He slipped from Iriya in the middle of the night, stepping into the cold, darkened courtyard outside of Quaver Castle and staring up at the way the moon hung in a low crescent smile beyond it.

It was cold and the castle had become quiet beneath the horrors they had experienced. Where sirens were known for their frivolity that could last well into the night hours, the halls of the castle resonated with a soft and foreboding silence. There were few people in his way, as he first moved to the Princess' bedroom, only to find it undisturbed, the bedsheets tucked in tight, and the pillows fluffed. The princess' soft scent was fading as if she had not been present in days.

Death grit his teeth and turned back to the castle and prowled through the stone halls to hunt her down.

27

Her screams of frustration bounced off the walls of the cold dungeon, falling on deaf ears, as she wailed until she was hoarse, demanding that they listen. The siren guards and the three Fae Princelings didn't turn, ignoring her as astutely that she couldn't help but wonder if she had turned invisible once again.

It was only the rough grumblings of the other prisoners that kept her sure that she still existed, could be seen and heard.

"Shut up!" One shouted, flinging a stale loaf of bread at the bars between their cells. "We don't wanna hear you whinging!"

"You shut up! You shut up!" Keziah screamed back, frenzied with panic and emotion, but her magic did not rise with it. It felt dull, hidden behind the barriers created by this prison. Walls lined with a soft blue moonstone, known to disable siren powers, the failsafe in case any siren, especially a Quaver, became too greedy or took too much.

There were no shackles on her wrists, her ankles, and they had not chained her to the wall like some of the other prisoners, but the cell was enough to dampen her completely. Without her magic, she had nothing. She was nothing.

"I want to speak to Kalani!" she screamed again. "I want to speak to my sister!"

"That's Queen Kalani to you!" One of the siren guards slammed his baton against the bars, and Keziah flinched back instinctively at the noise. "And you'll take my queen's name from your mouth, you treasonous sirret!"

He spat through the bars, and it landed on her bare feet.

Keziah wanted to cry, for as forgotten and invisible as she had felt before, she had never experienced such disrespect at the hands of the guards; but they had stolen her diadem, removing the marker of her royal blood before they threw her into the cells like any other siren.

Tadhg appeared at the bars and laid a hand on the guard's shoulder. He squeezed gently, a firm warning for the male to leave. The fae remained at the bars, though, peering through them at the siren within.

"Your Queen has stated you will remain here, without contact with your court, until the Ash are prepared to transfer you to our prison awaiting sentencing."

Keziah trembled, her bottom lip dropping, looking up at him beneath dark, wet lashes. "But..."

"Don't try me with that siren gaze, Princess," His voice was rough, tense, as if he were withholding himself from violence. "You murdered my brother. That's unforgivable."

"I didn't mean to!" Keziah assured him quickly, running for the bars. She wrapped her hands around his, skin against skin, and he scowled, pulling himself free. "I didn't mean to hurt him, I swear it! I swear it on the Queen's life!"

It was the ultimate oath for the sirens, those who beloved their queens, the source of their power, but Tadhg simply rose a single brow and watched her with an unimpressed grimace.

"Who are you to swear on queens, Keziah of Quaver?" He asked ominously. "When you have killed one of them, too."

She said nothing; bowing her head until dark curls obscured her face. Her silence condemned her; hot tears rolled down her cheeks and dripped from her chin.

Tadhg backed away from the bars, turning to his brothers and leaving her to her misery.

Quietly he had slipped past the guards and the princes, in the middle of the night. When Keziah looked up from her tears, scrubbing her ringed fingers across her tired face, he was standing in the shadows of the cell, face impassive, gaze dark.

She stumbled to her feet, but when she approached Death took a swift step back. The dark anger on his face froze her in place.

"Are you mad?" Keziah whispered.

His nostrils flared, a cold fury in his features that meant the question required no genuine answer. Of course, he was mad. She had killed one of his own. Misery welled in her gut, sharp and bitter, at the thought that she had disappointed him.

"Why?" Death asked.

"Why did I kill them?" Keziah clarified, confused.

"Why," He corrected sharply. "Do you care if I'm mad at you, Princess?"

The sigh she released was heavy, weighed with thought and doubt. Keziah twisted her fingers in her skirts and looked up at him through lowered lashes. "Because you matter to me..."

He scoffed, a derisive sound. "Hardly."

She stamped her foot; the sound dull against the cold stone floor. "Because I want you to notice me, but I also want you to like me. It's important."

"I don't like you," He stated.

Keziah flinched. "Liar."

"You dare look in the face of Death and call him a liar?" The fae hissed, advancing on her quickly, and Keziah backed until he had trapped in the corner of her room. Her grey eyes flicked through the bars to assess her fellow prisoners, but she couldn't look away from him for long.

She lifted her chin, full lips parted, and dared to speak. "You don't need to like me to want me, Death. I see you, the real you, beneath the shadows."

He inhaled sharply, lips thinning with anger.

"You're not so different from the rest of us," Keziah continued boldly. "We're the same, you and me. We're so lonely. We just want people to see us, but I see you. Really, I do. Take me with you, Death, to wherever it is you call home..."

He laughed, a dark sound that caused the guards to rustle. "You want me to steal you away, princess?"

"Yes!" she cried.

Death laughed in her face. "I came to punish you, Keziah of Quaver, for the torment you've caused me."

"Oh." Keziah wanted to sob. The air felt thin in her lungs, as she realised that the dark fae who stoles in the quiets moments after passing may not be her saviour.

He stepped close again, his hands wreathed with shadows as he reached to caress her jaw. His soft fingers caressed the curve of her jaw, causing Keziah's breath to hitch, and a soft sigh to slip free of her lips again.

"The best punishment," Death whispered, leaning close, his breath cool as it washed over her lips, and she caught herself wishing he would close that gap and kiss her just once. "Is to leave to face the consequences of your actions."

He let go, quickly putting space between them, and Keziah lurched after him. Death's solemn smile was sharp as he bowed his head. "I hope you survive it, Keziah of Quaver, or I'll be seeing you sooner than we both desire."

The world seemed to ripple around him as despair rippled inside of her chest. There was a fissure starting at her heart and cracking her wide open.

"You won't leave me!" She howled. "I am yours and you are mine!"

Keziah grappled with her emotions, struggling to think, struggling to breathe, as she parted her lips and screamed after death again, soft lilting words in an ancient siren language, a series of haunted notes flowing from her lips, an old song of death. Used in the times before sirens took the land to lure souls to their peril in the depths of icy waters.

She sought not to kill him, but to capture him, to keep death by her side as a companion in the lonely days. He was hers, and he would see as much if only he gave her a little time.

Death paused on the precipice between two worlds, turning back to look at the siren, listen to the call of her deadly song.

The surrounding prisoners stopped breathing, and their souls screamed with agony; the guards slumped lifeless to the floor and the fae princes struggled to ignore the call, dropping to their knees, fingers clawing at their hearts as they squeezed tight beneath the siren song.

Their hearts stopped; their lives ended too easily.

Death watched in horror as Keziah killed them all.

28

The power of the ancient siren song threatened to still the beat of his own stony heart. Death grit his teeth, glaring down at the powerful mistress who sung for his attention, who called for his Death and growled back with equal power.

He had told her she was powerful, thinking she was no more so than her predecessors, but the well of emotion and raw magic she had tapped was well beyond what he could have imagined. She was dangerous.

"Enough!" Death growled, stepping back into Solis long enough to wrap shadows around them both, silencing the reach of her song before it could extend to the rest of the castle, and she could send the entirety of Quaver Castle and the three siren courts to Iriya. He feared it would reach even beyond that. "That is enough, Keziah!"

The shadows spun like a tornado; and her power compacted around them. His heart skipped a beat, painful in his chest, and it reminded Death that he was not as infallible as he pretended to be. The faces of Death had come and gone before him, and his time might come too soon, at the hands of an underestimated siren.

He forced her backwards, carried by the shadows, and reached for her face. "Stop it!" Death seethed at the siren who still sung, stubborn and filled with relentless power. Her body glowed as if the sun had birthed in her heart, her song strengthened with every being that fell at her command.

She was a creature of death; just like him.

"I'm here," He growled at her, changing his tact, but while her grey eyes glittered, they showed no recognition of his presence or his words. His hands pressed against her cheeks, warm beneath his palms, the magic in her veins thrumming at his touch.

He swallowed, conflicted, and then pressed her against the wall, tilting her chin back and sealing his mouth across her full lips, swallowing every note of her siren song beneath his kiss.

It poisoned him from the inside out, but he held tight, his fingers digging into her soft flesh, anchoring himself to her and her back to him while he consumed the song. She meant to kill an entire realm.

Keziah ran out of breath and stopped singing; At the end of her song, he let go. Death fell to the floor, not unlike her other victims, while the Siren Princess watched on with a troubled, tear-filled gaze.

Her fingers raised to her lips, touching them softly.

Death's head knocked against the concrete with a crack as his body spasmed with uncontrollable seizures. He could feel the trickle of hot blood running down his neck. The shadows slipping around him, binding tight to his skin as they attempted to exile the poison of the sirens' magic.

He twisted, rolling in on himself, before his body forced him to retch, repeatedly, until he vomited black sludge across the marble floor. A physical manifestation of the rot she had been inducing. Sweat beaded across his brow, his hair sticking to his skin as his body trembled again, eyes rolling into his skull as a seizure wracked his body.

Keziah said nothing, only whimpering softly, her breathing heavy and her eyes wide as she watched him fight for his life.

Death groaned loudly. He rolled onto his stomach, using the last vestiges of energy to drag himself across the cold stone floor. His fingers outstretched, reaching for his discarded scythe.

He gripped the opal handle tightly, a strangled groan of pain echoing around them both as Death tore a hole between the two realms and tumbled into the safety of Iriya.

He landed on his back in the middle of the Triplean Fields, by the thermal springs, a place of healing for the souls of his world. His lungs spasmed, and he struggled to breathe, sure that her song would take him even after all this effort.

Pain shot through his body, numbing his legs as he used his arms to drag himself into the steaming water, slipping over the edge and tumbling below the surface.

Souls hovered at the edge of the lake, screaming as Death did not rise from the water. Shadow and Light bobbed at the edges of the springs, taking form, with large wings spread behind their backs.

"Give him room," Jael roared.

Yael bristled and snapped, "Don't talk to my souls like that!"

They lingered by the edge of the steaming water, peering into the dark depths as they waited for Death to rise. Iriya rumbled precariously beneath their feet, stones dislodging from the cliffs that surrounded them, tumbling into the water.

The shadows of light and darkness shared an intense look, features turning grave.

"Perhaps it was his time to die, Jael," the angel of light whispered softly.

"No!" The rebuke came not from her dark counterpart, but through the tear in the realms that slowly repaired, leaving a small portal between Solis and Iriya. "He can't die on me."

The realm trembled again as Keziah, siren princess of Solis, stepped through the rift between the realms and landed, barefoot and tear-stained, in the Triplean Fields.

The realm shook, rejecting the living soul. Yael and Jael both backed away, reaching for the souls that surrounded them, shepherding them away from the taint in their realm.

"Where is he?" Keziah cried; voice strained. "Tell me!"

The silence was deafening, but she followed their gazes to the depths of the water, and without hesitating, she dove into the hot waters.

It pressed against her, overwhelming and dragging her down. She could see him beneath the surface, sinking towards the ground. Keziah kicked as hard as she could, reaching for him, desperately wrapping her hands in his clothing, and trying to kick her way back to the surface.

His white hair floated around his head like a halo, his skin pale, his weight too heavy for her to bear, but somehow Keziah found the strength to bring him to the surface.

They broke through the water, and sweet, frigid air filled her lungs.

Strong arms wrapped around them both as the angels of light and darkness pulled them from the springs and dragged them into the soft grass.

Keziah coughed, choking on the drops of water that had invaded her lungs; she sat up, sucking in deep breaths of precious air. She forced her tired body to shift, crawling through the grass to where Death lay, his white hair fanned across the ground, his chest unmoving.

"No!" She reached him, pushing against his side, rolling him until she could thump her hand against his back. "No! No!! You will wake up; you will wake up!"

There was magic in those words, in the desperate and broken plea, but his body spasmed one last time, and Death vomited water and sludge onto the grass.

The surrounding souls began to whisper, their voices rising in volume as the seconds ticked by. When Death slowly opened his eyes, Jael and Yael knelt in the grass, bowing low, not to him, but to the soaked siren by his side.

"All Hail the Queen of Death."

Acknowledgements

Thank you to everyone who has once more supported me through a whole another project and the creation of a new world with The Four Realms.

To Emily, for being my first beta-reader and the first to dive into the story of Keziah and Death. Thank you for your thoughts, you have no idea how much it means to me.

Alana, Jasmin, Bailee, Samantha, Tierney and more for completing a "vibe check" to see how Death's Stalker might appeal to an audience; and being willing to go in blind for me.

Ira, who waited patiently for each walk as I finished one more line.

Rhys, who cooked too many dinners while I was writing and listened to every plot-hole with patience, even if he had no idea what was happening.

'The Second Cup' Writers Community, keep kicking goals! I've loved having peers to chat with throughout, your support is everything.

About the Author

Stephanie Gluck writes on the traditional lands of the Larrakia and Dunghutti people and pays her respects to Elders past, present, and emerging.

When Stephanie isn't writing she avidly feeds her coffee addiction and adds to her ever-growing collection of books (most of which still need to be read). She is a Registered Nurse and lives in the Australia with her partner Rhys, and Great Dane, Ira.

You can keep up to date with Stephanie and her upcoming work at www.stephaniegluck.com

www.ingramcontent.com/pod-product-compliance
Lightning Source LLC
Chambersburg PA
CBHW030523120726
47904CB00005B/1602